COOKIE & BROCCOLI

READY FOR SCHOOL!

Bob McMahon

Dial Books for  Young Readers

Warning!
This is a
very silly
book!

For Lalane and Tyler, who keep this
Cookie from crumbling

DIAL BOOKS FOR YOUNG READERS

An imprint of Penguin Random House LLC, New York

Visit us online at penguinrandomhouse.com

Library of Congress Cataloging-in-Publication Data is available.

Printed in China

ISBN 9780593109076

2 4 6 8 10 9 7 5 3 1

Design by Jennifer Kelly

Text handlettered by the author

This artwork was created digitally using Corel Painter
and by eating lots of chocolate.

CONTENTS

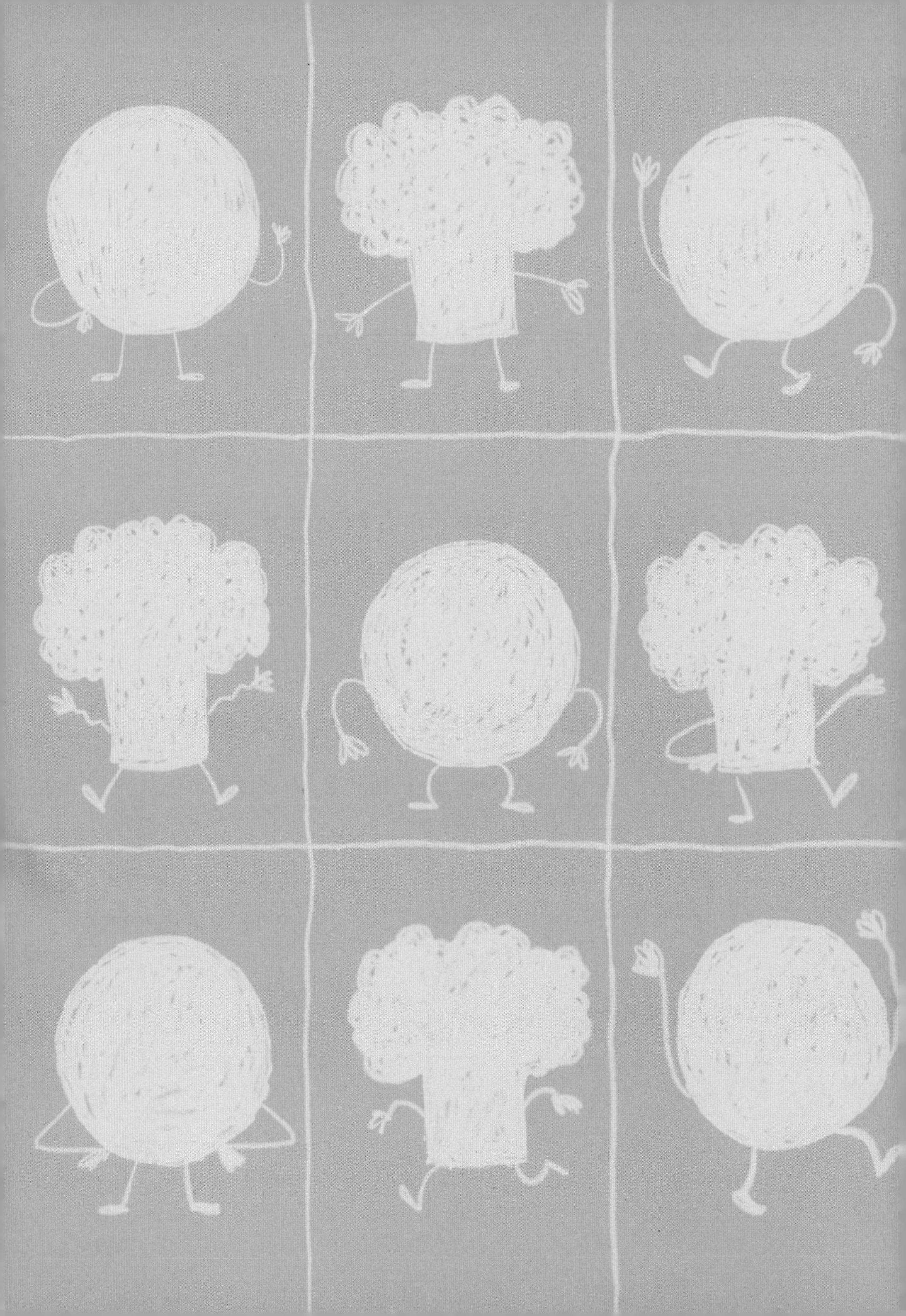

Chapter 1

HOW WE MET!

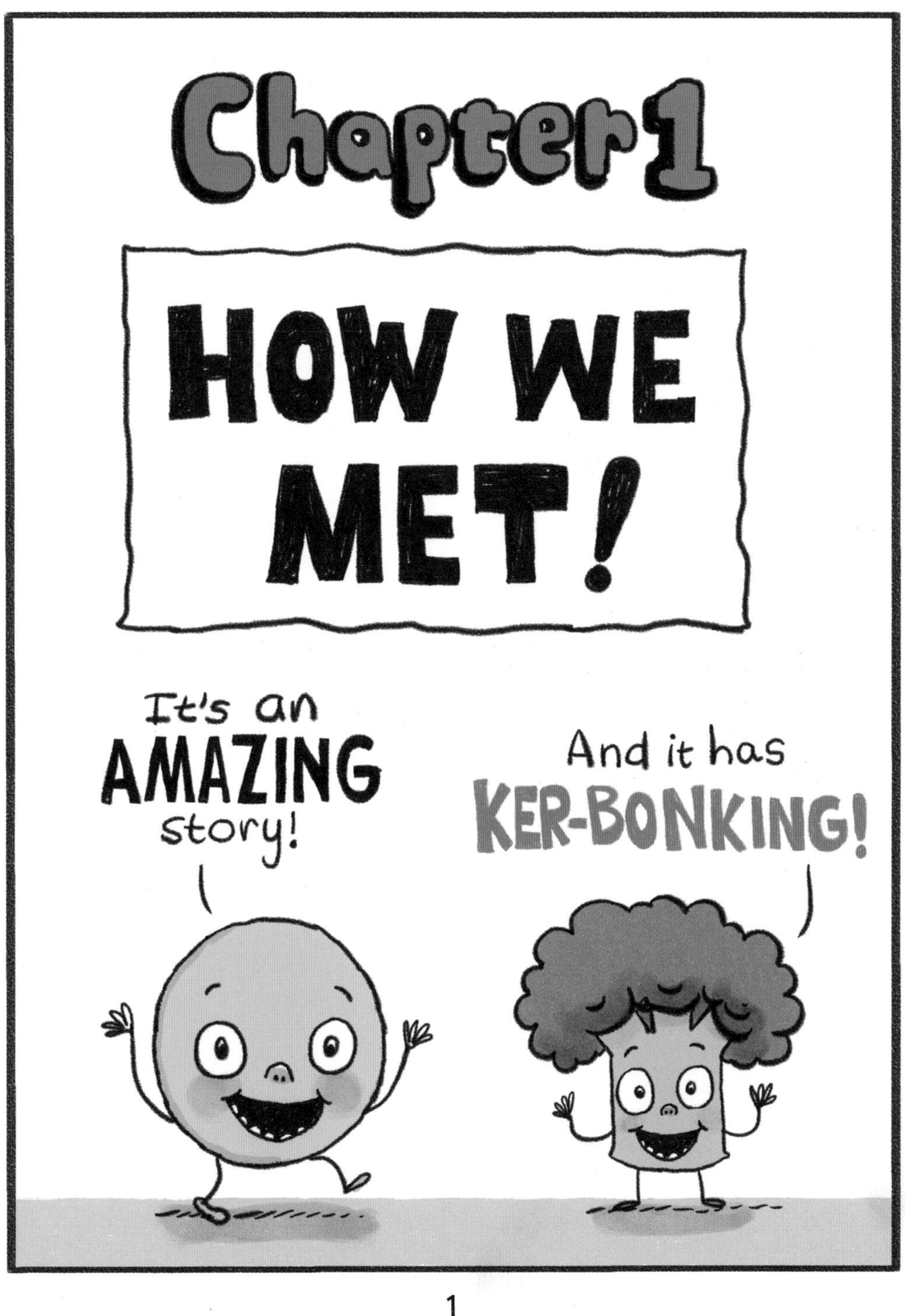
It's an AMAZING story!
And it has KER-BONKING!

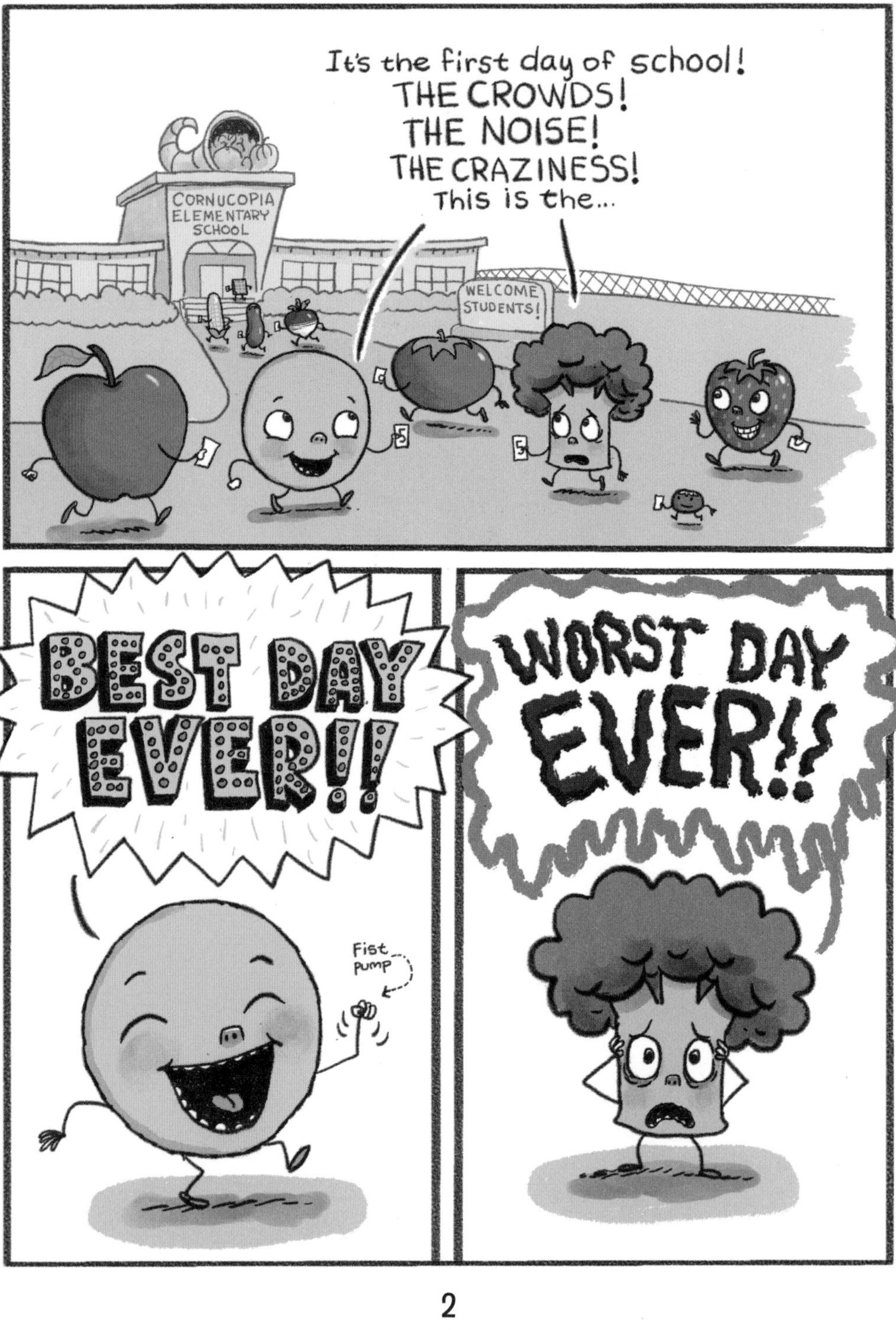
It's the first day of school!
THE CROWDS!
THE NOISE!
THE CRAZINESS!
This is the...
CORNUCOPIA ELEMENTARY SCHOOL
WELCOME STUDENTS!
BEST DAY EVER!!
Fist pump
WORST DAY EVER!?

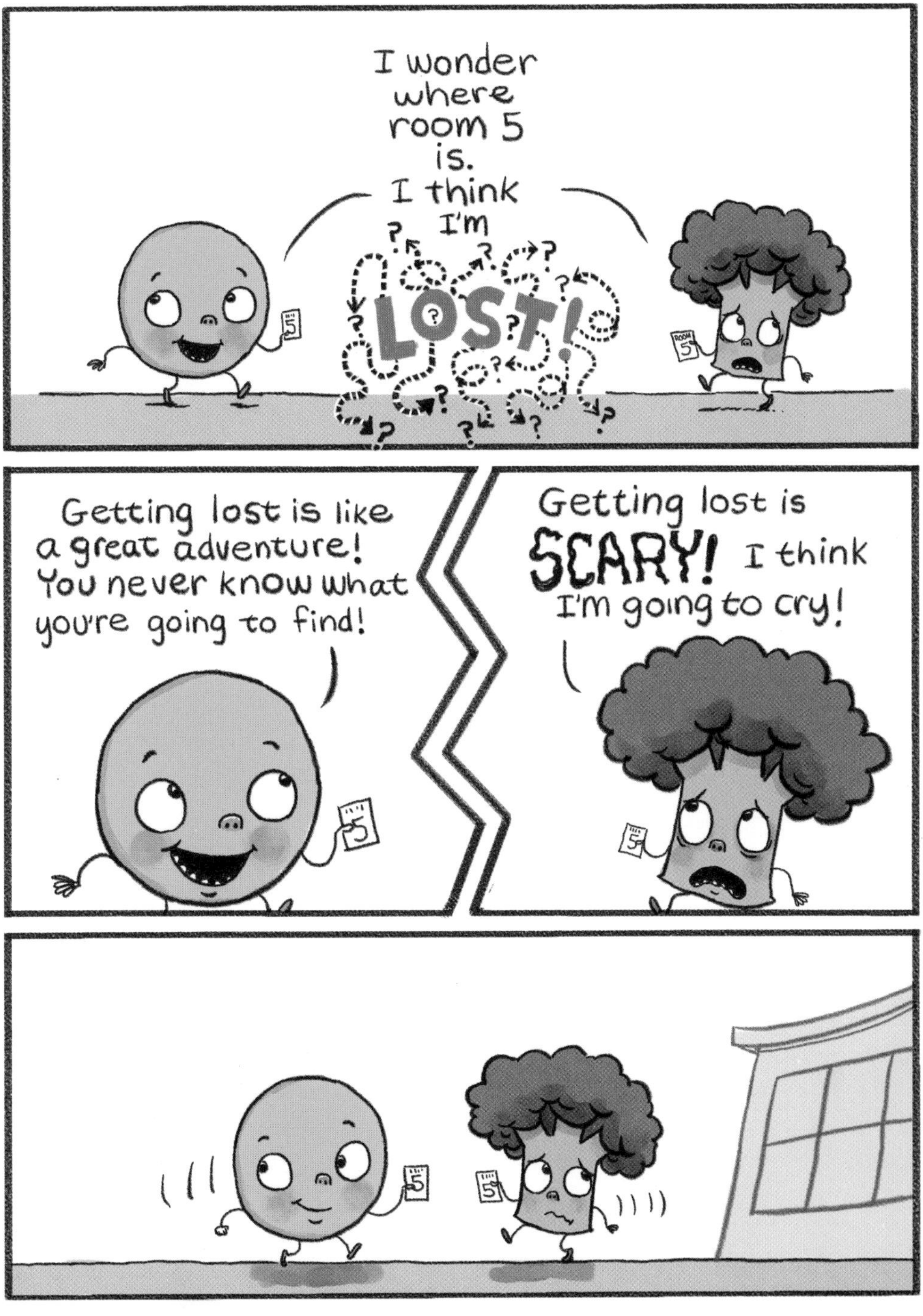

I wonder where room 5 is. I think I'm
LOST!
Getting lost is like a great adventure! You never know what you're going to find!
Getting lost is SCARY! I think I'm going to cry!

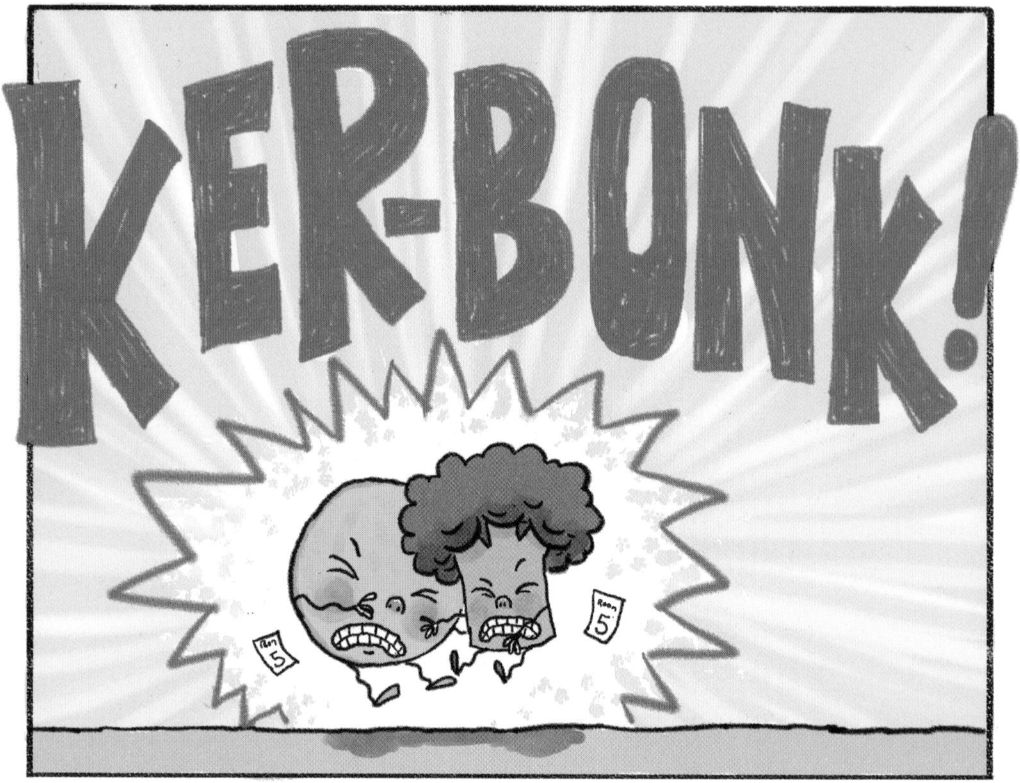
KER-BONK!

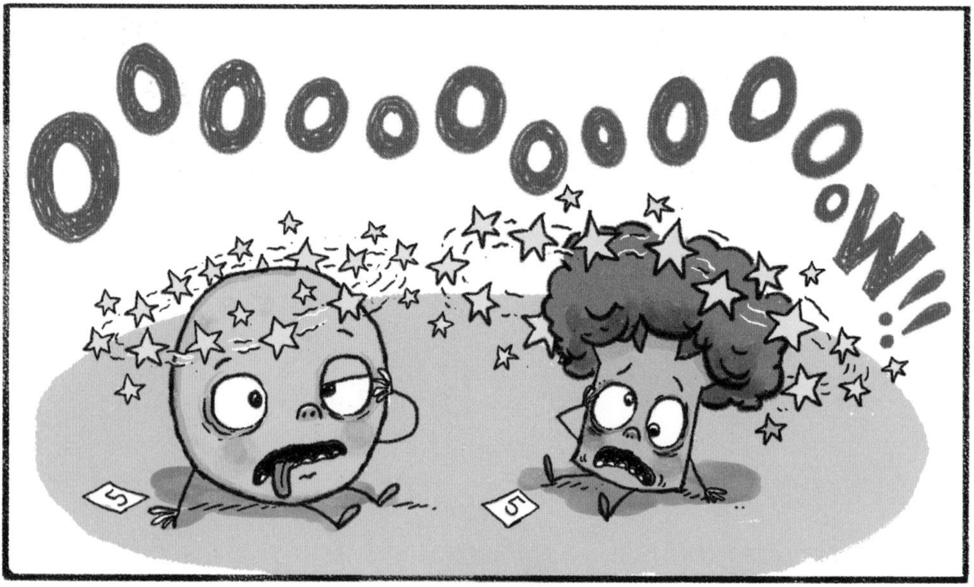
OOOOOOOOOOOOW!!

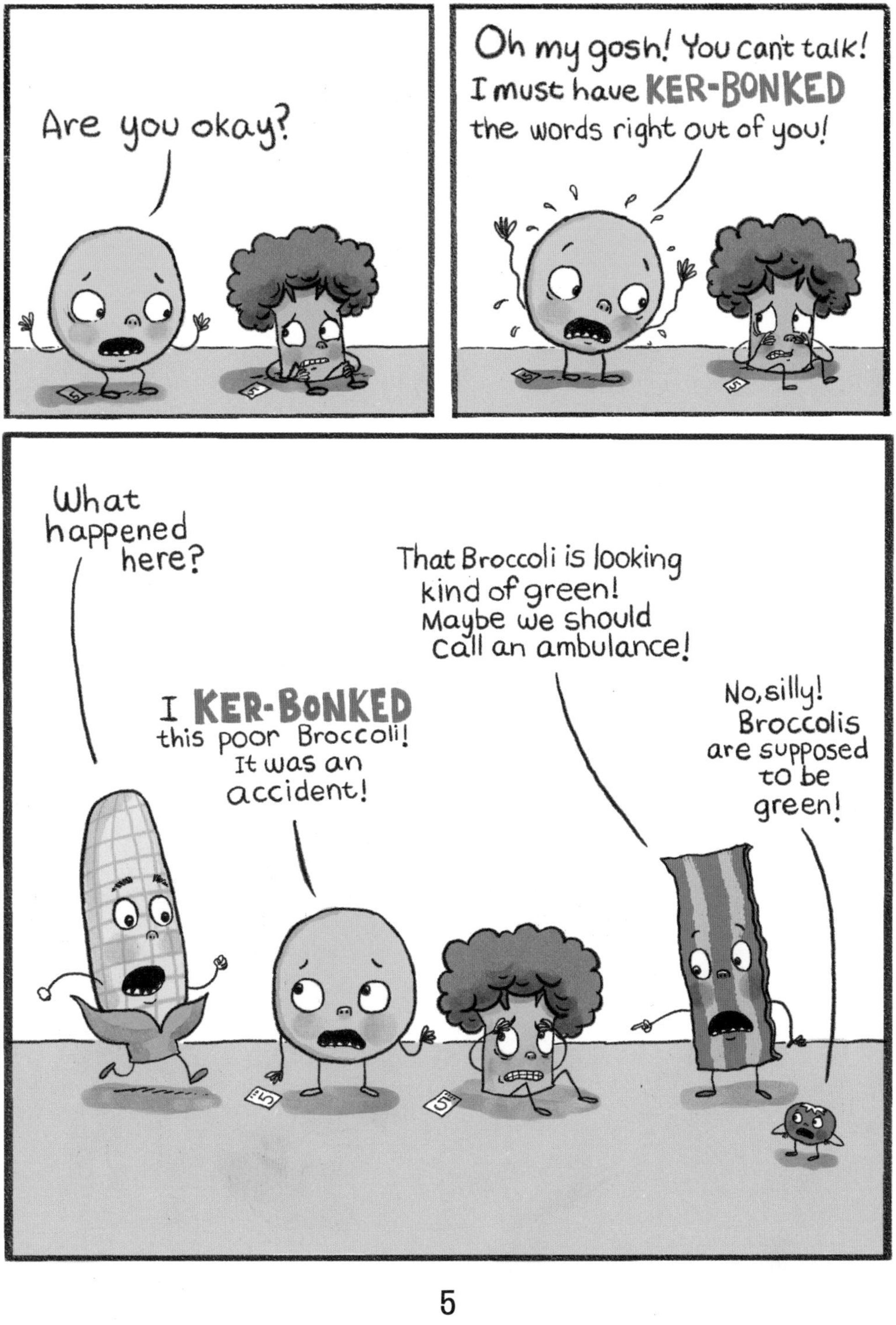

Are you okay?
Oh my gosh! You can't talk! I must have KER-BONKED the words right out of you!
What happened here?
I KER-BONKED this poor Broccoli! It was an accident!
That Broccoli is looking kind of green! Maybe we should call an ambulance!
No, silly! Broccolis are supposed to be green!

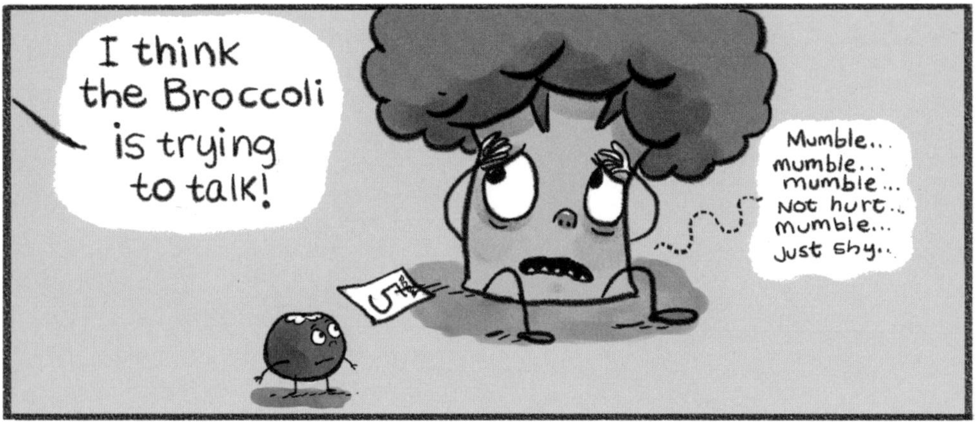
I think the Broccoli is trying to talk!
Mumble... mumble... mumble... Not hurt... Mumble... Just shy...

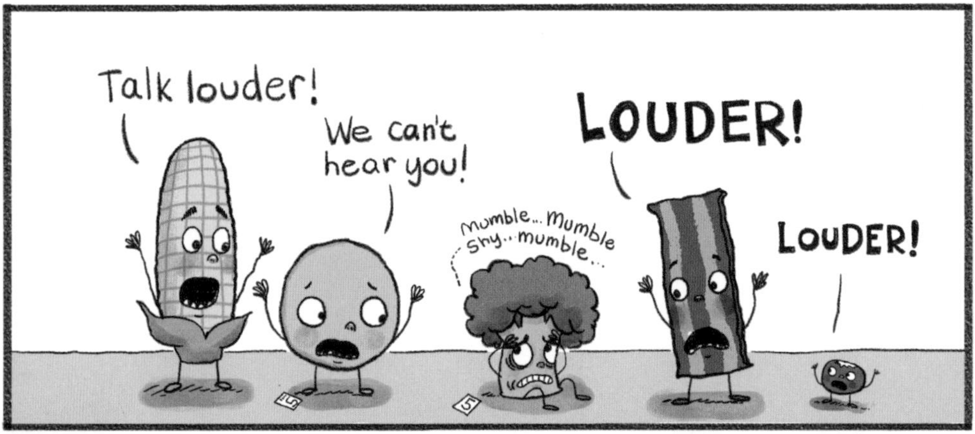
Talk louder!
We can't hear you!
Mumble... Mumble Shy... mumble...
LOUDER!
LOUDER!

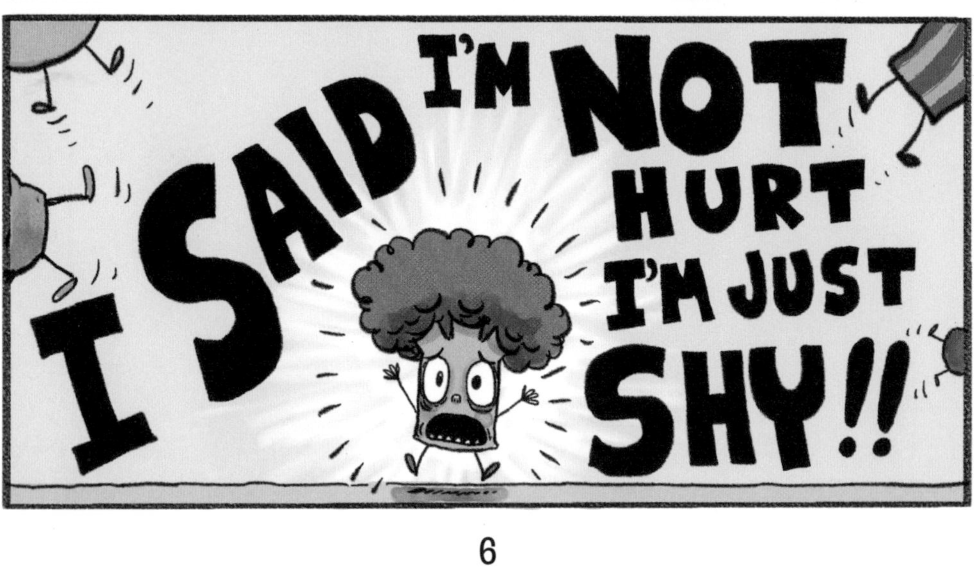
I SAID I'M NOT HURT I'M JUST SHY!!

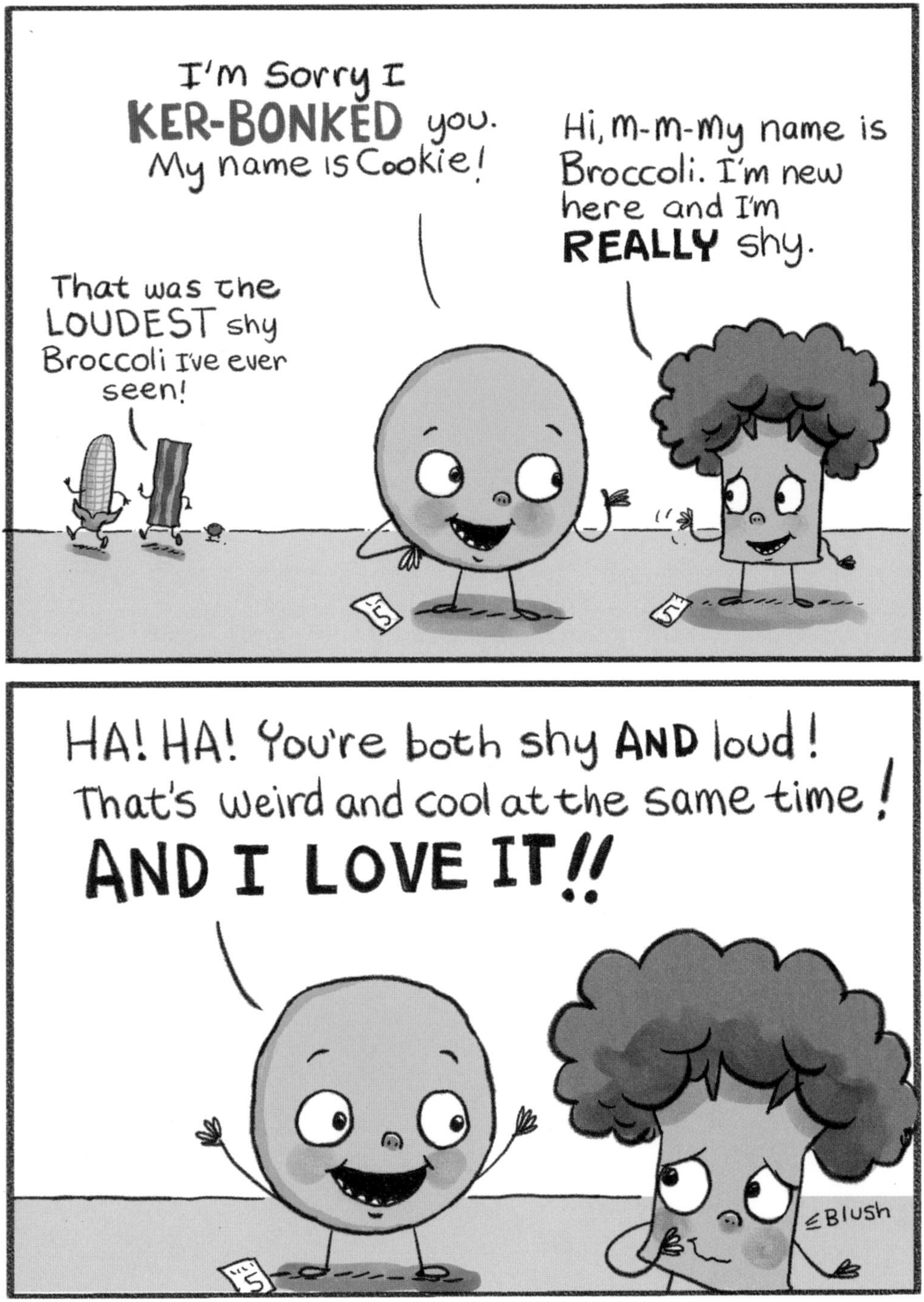
I'm Sorry I KER-BONKED you. My name is Cookie!
Hi, m-m-my name is Broccoli. I'm new here and I'm REALLY shy.
That was the LOUDEST shy Broccoli I've ever seen!
5
5
HA! HA! You're both shy AND loud! That's weird and cool at the same time! AND I LOVE IT!!
5
BLUSH

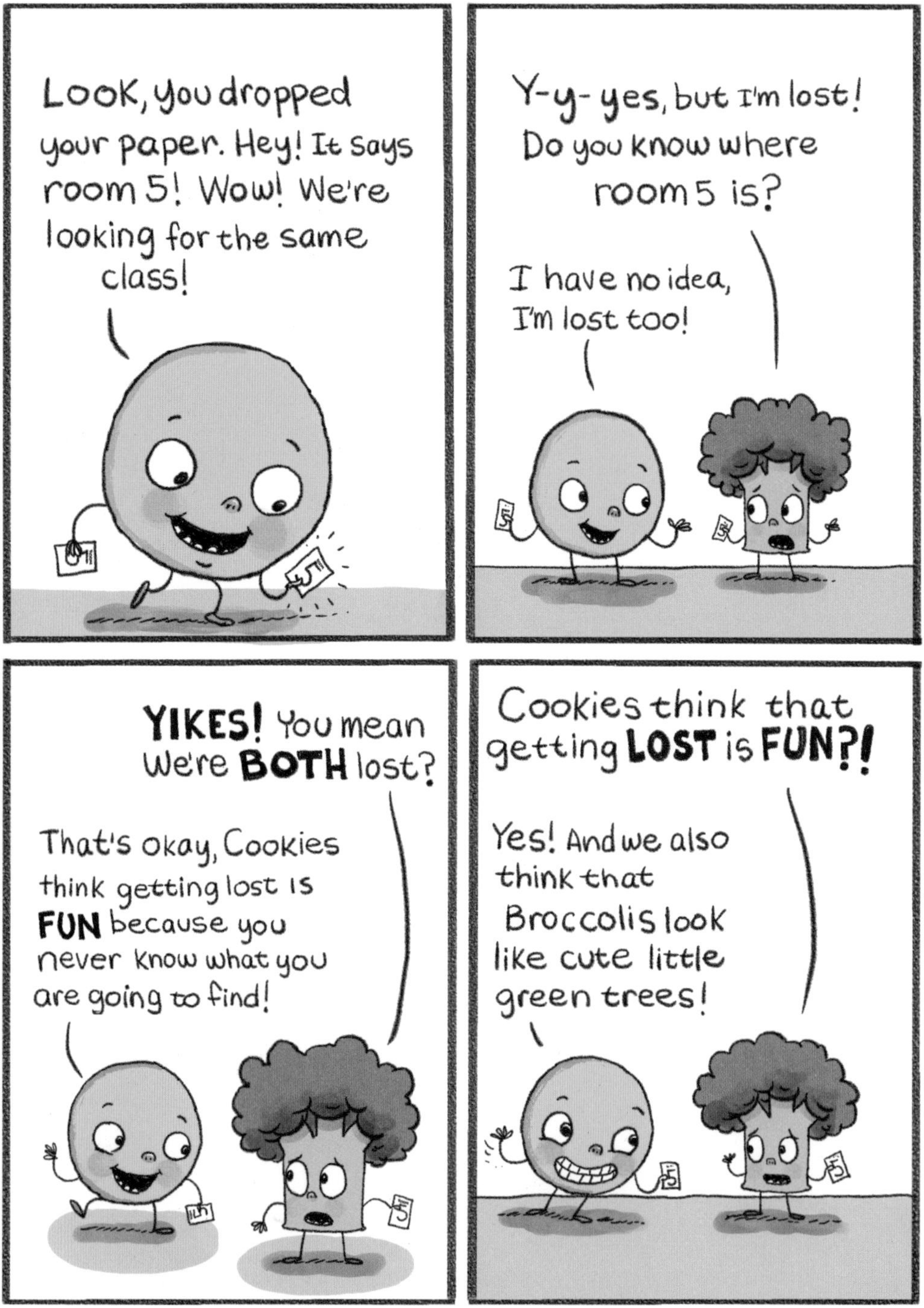
LOOK, you dropped your paper. Hey! It says room 5! Wow! We're looking for the same class!
Y-y- yes, but I'm lost! Do you know where room 5 is?
I have no idea, I'm lost too!
YIKES! You mean We're BOTH lost?
That's okay, Cookies think getting lost is FUN because you never know what you are going to find!
Cookies think that getting LOST is FUN?!
Yes! And we also think that Broccolis look like cute little green trees!

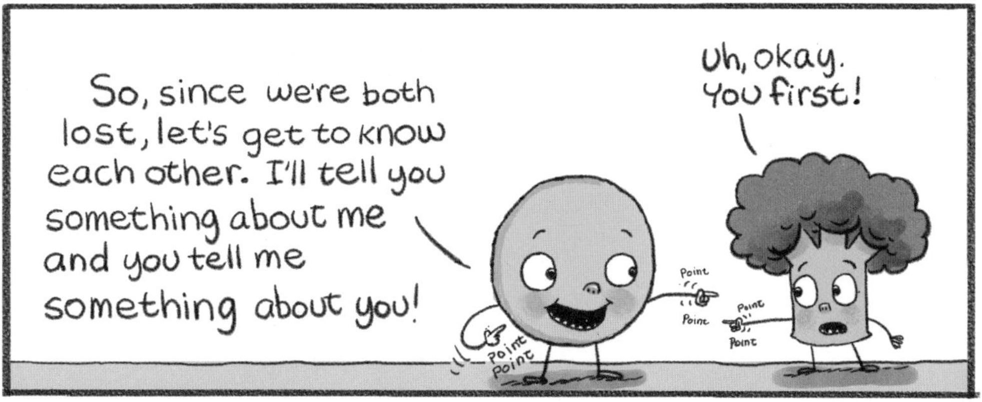
So, since we're both lost, let's get to know each other. I'll tell you something about me and you tell me something about you!
Point Point
Point Point
Uh, okay. You first!
Point Point

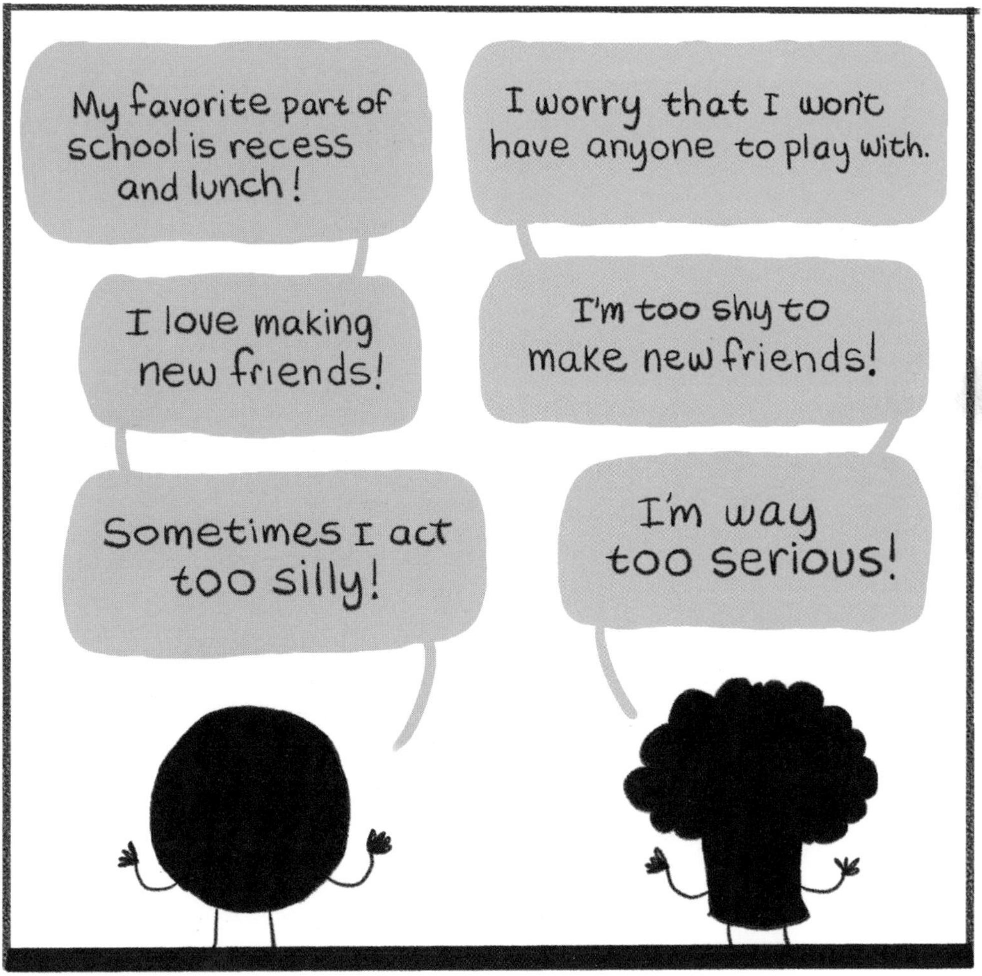
My favorite part of school is recess and lunch!
I love making new friends!
Sometimes I act too silly!
I worry that I won't have anyone to play with.
I'm too shy to make new friends!
I'm way too serious!

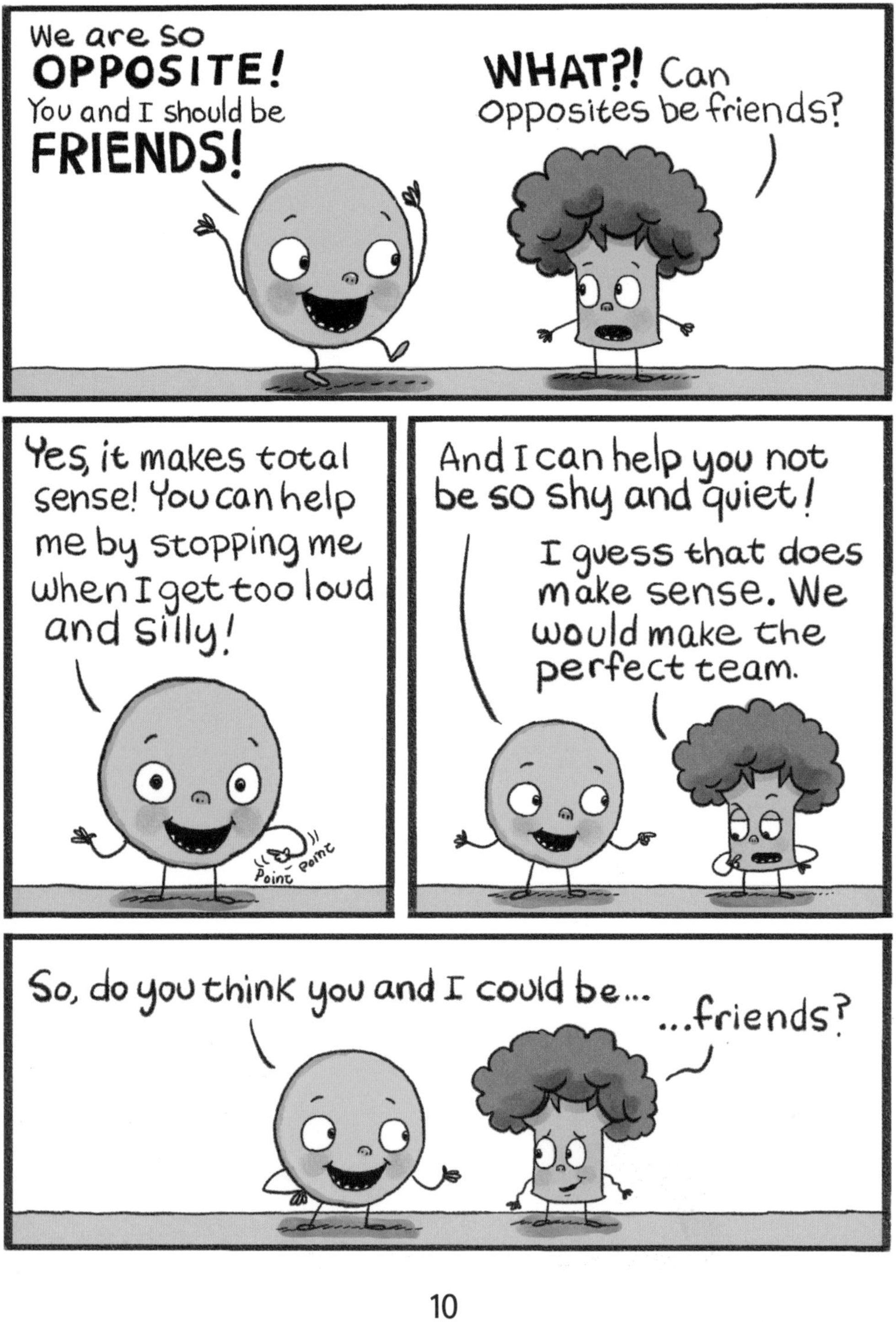
We are so OPPOSITE! You and I should be FRIENDS!
WHAT?! Can opposites be friends?
Yes, it makes total sense! You can help me by stopping me when I get too loud and silly!
Point Point
And I can help you not be so shy and quiet!
I guess that does make sense. We would make the perfect team.
So, do you think you and I could be...
...friends?

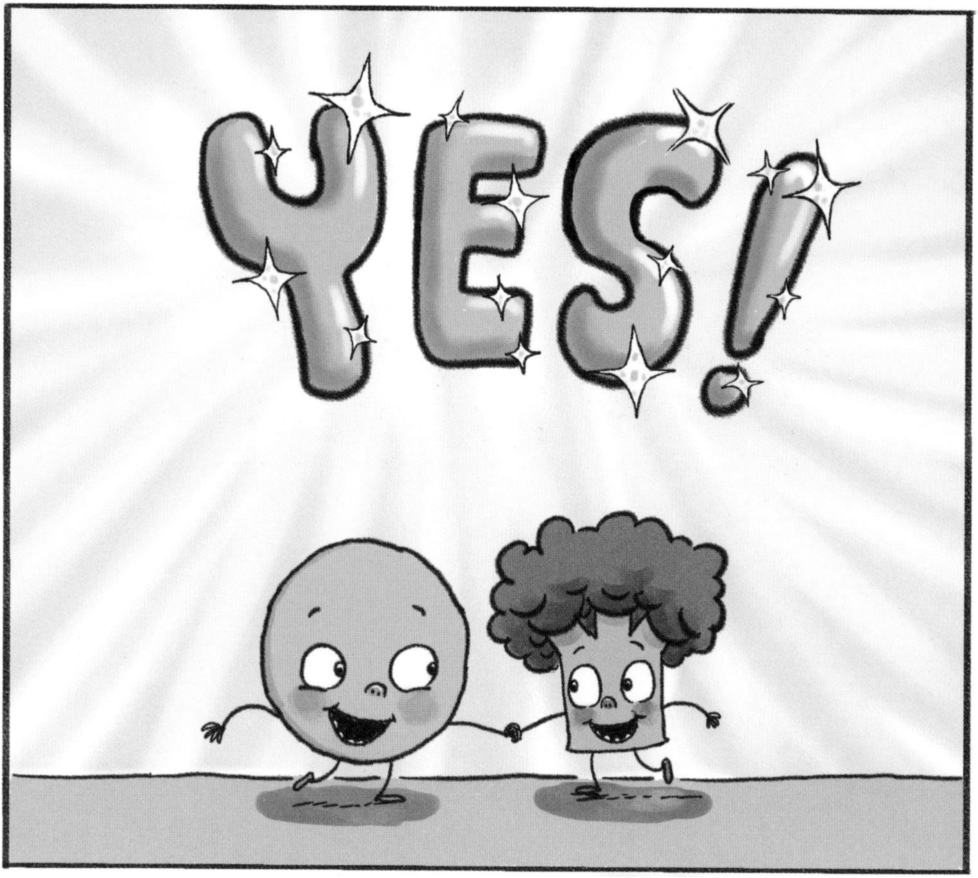
YES!

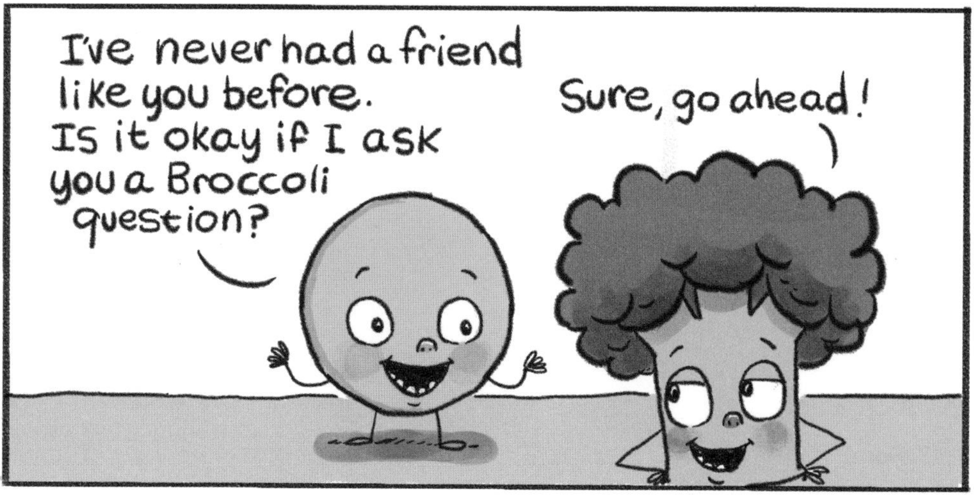
I've never had a friend like you before. Is it okay if I ask you a Broccoli question?
Sure, go ahead!

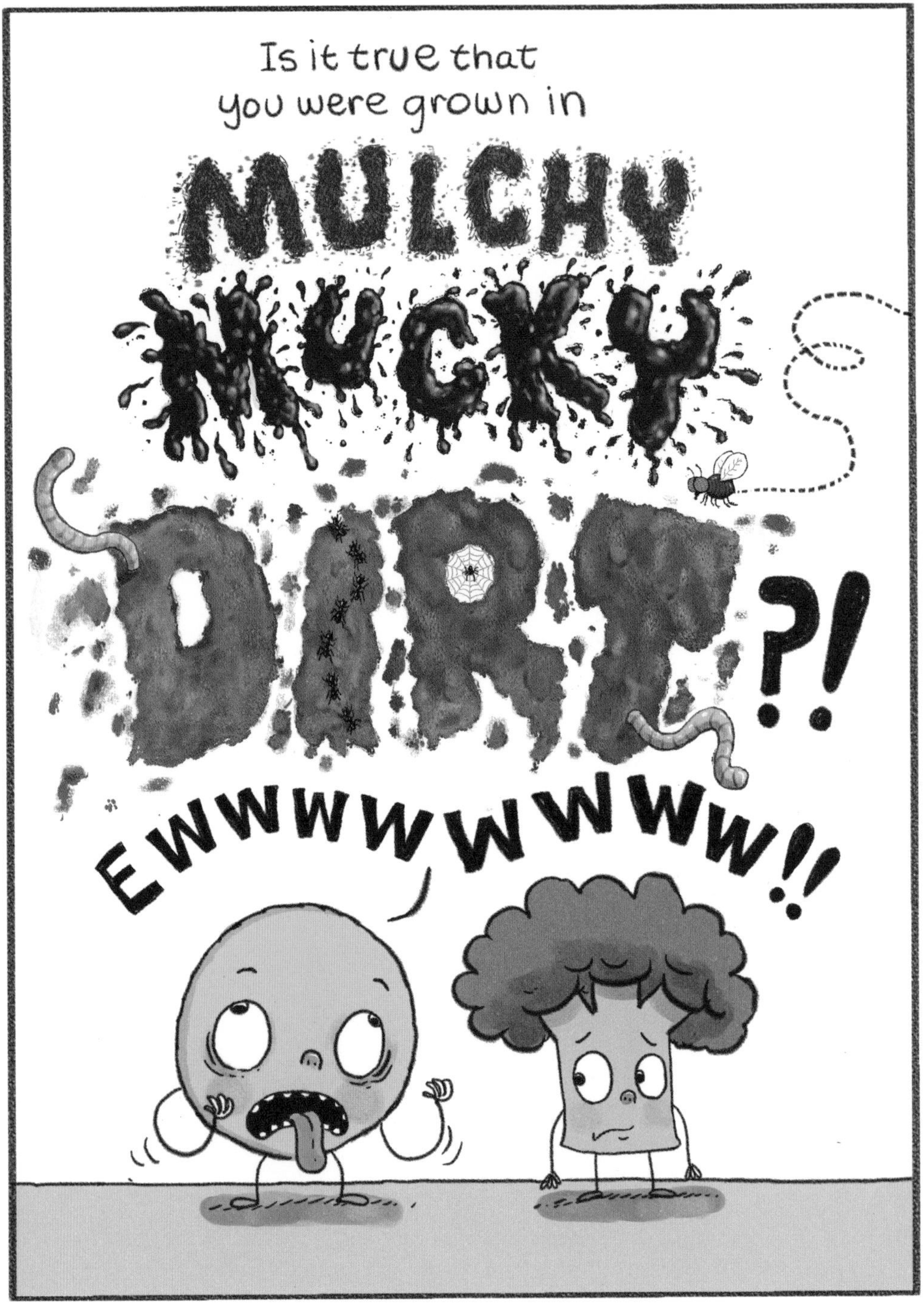
Is it true that you were grown in
MULCHY
MUCKY
DIRT?!
EWWWWWWWW!!

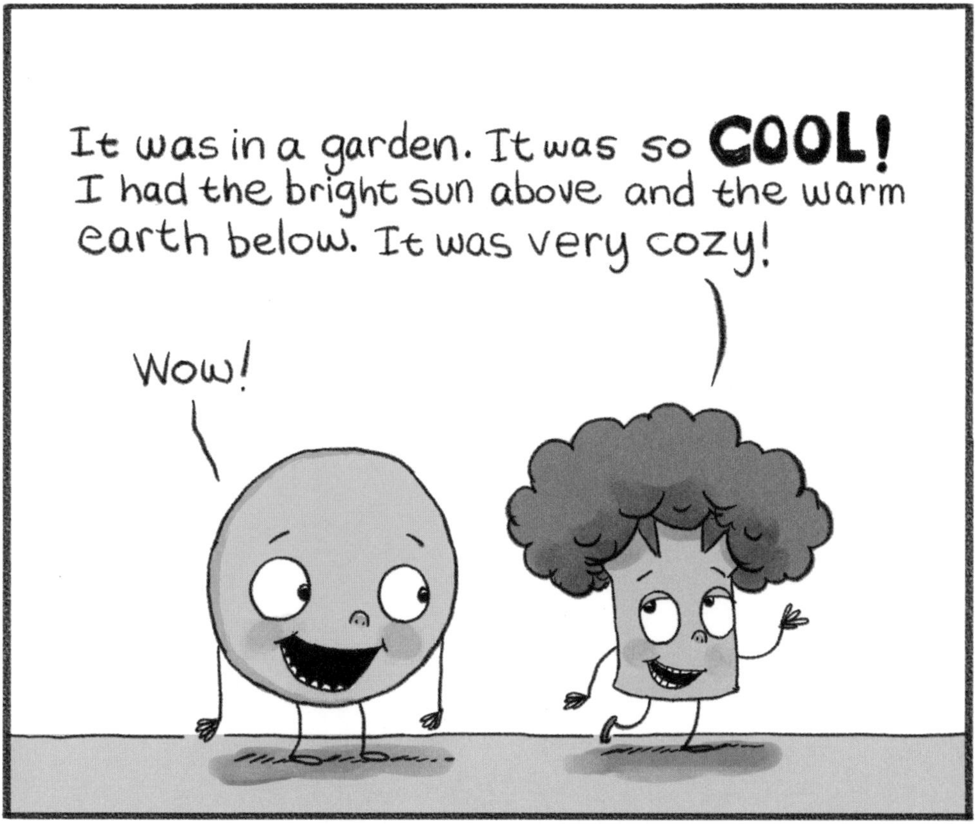
It was in a garden. It was so COOL! I had the bright sun above and the warm earth below. It was very cozy!
Wow!

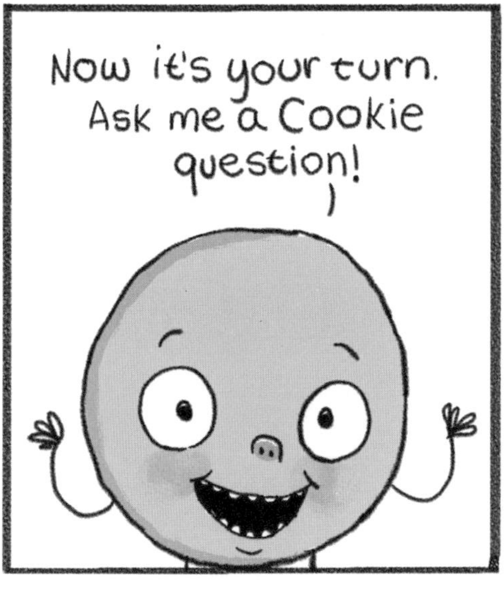
Now it's your turn. Ask me a Cookie question!

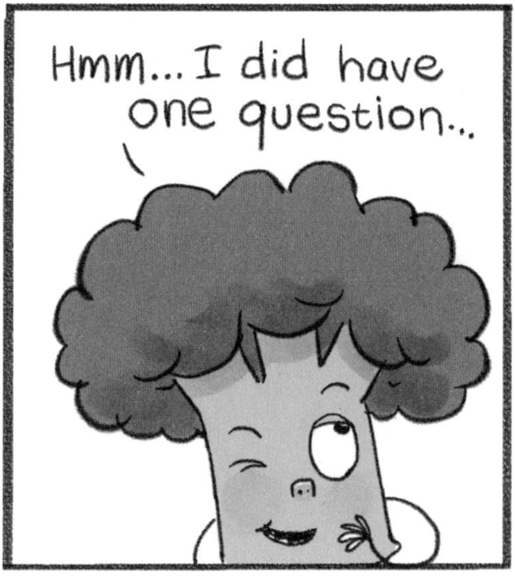
Hmm... I did have one question...

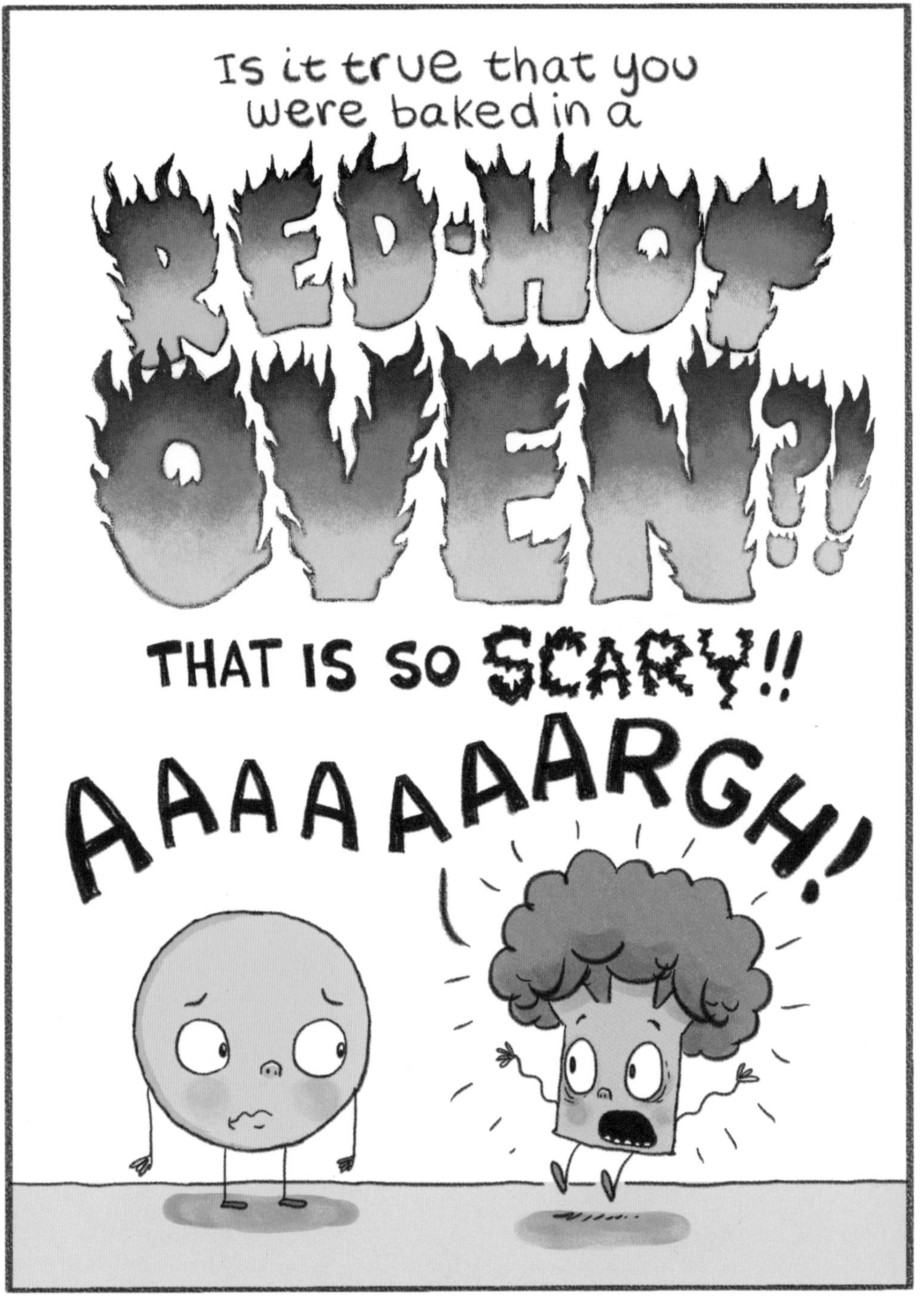
Is it true that you were baked in a
RED-HOT OVEN?!
THAT IS SO SCARY!!
AAAAAAARGH!

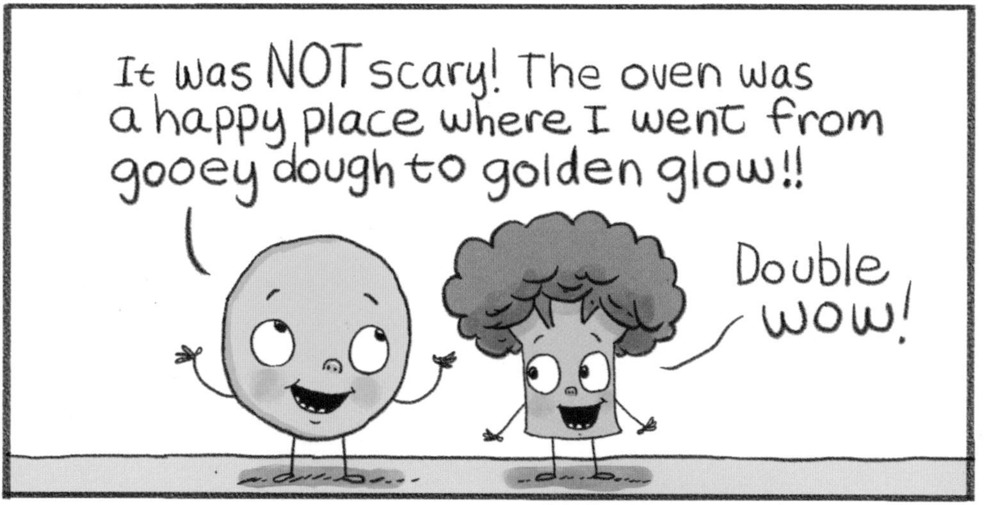
It was NOT scary! The oven was a happy place where I went from gooey dough to golden glow!!
Double wow!

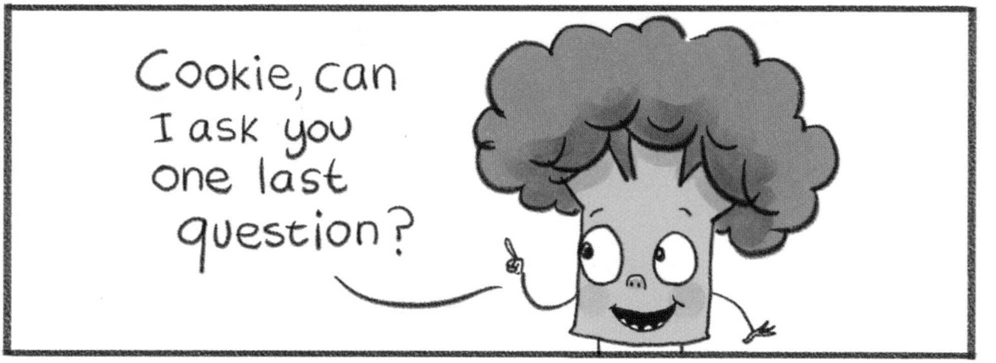
Cookie, can I ask you one last question?

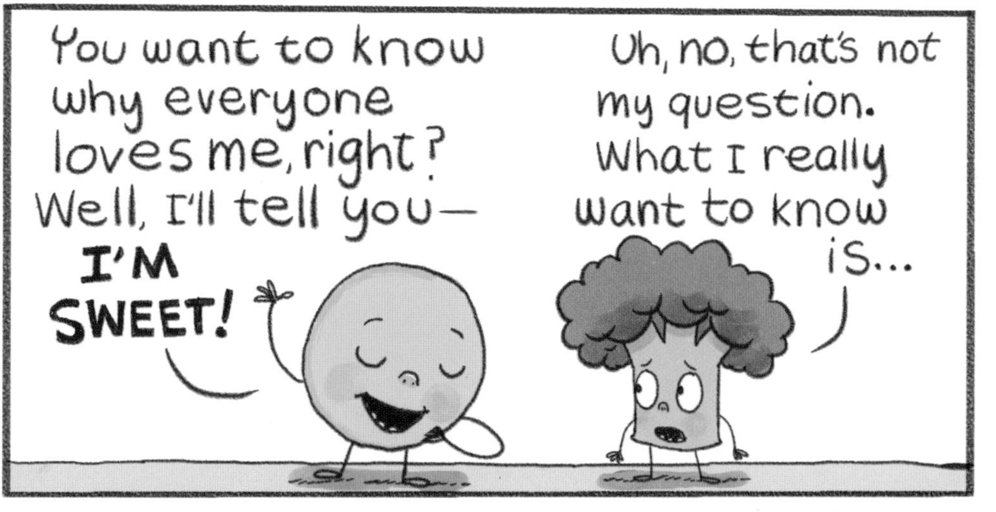
You want to know why everyone loves me, right? Well, I'll tell you—
I'M SWEET!
Uh, no, that's not my question. What I really want to know is...

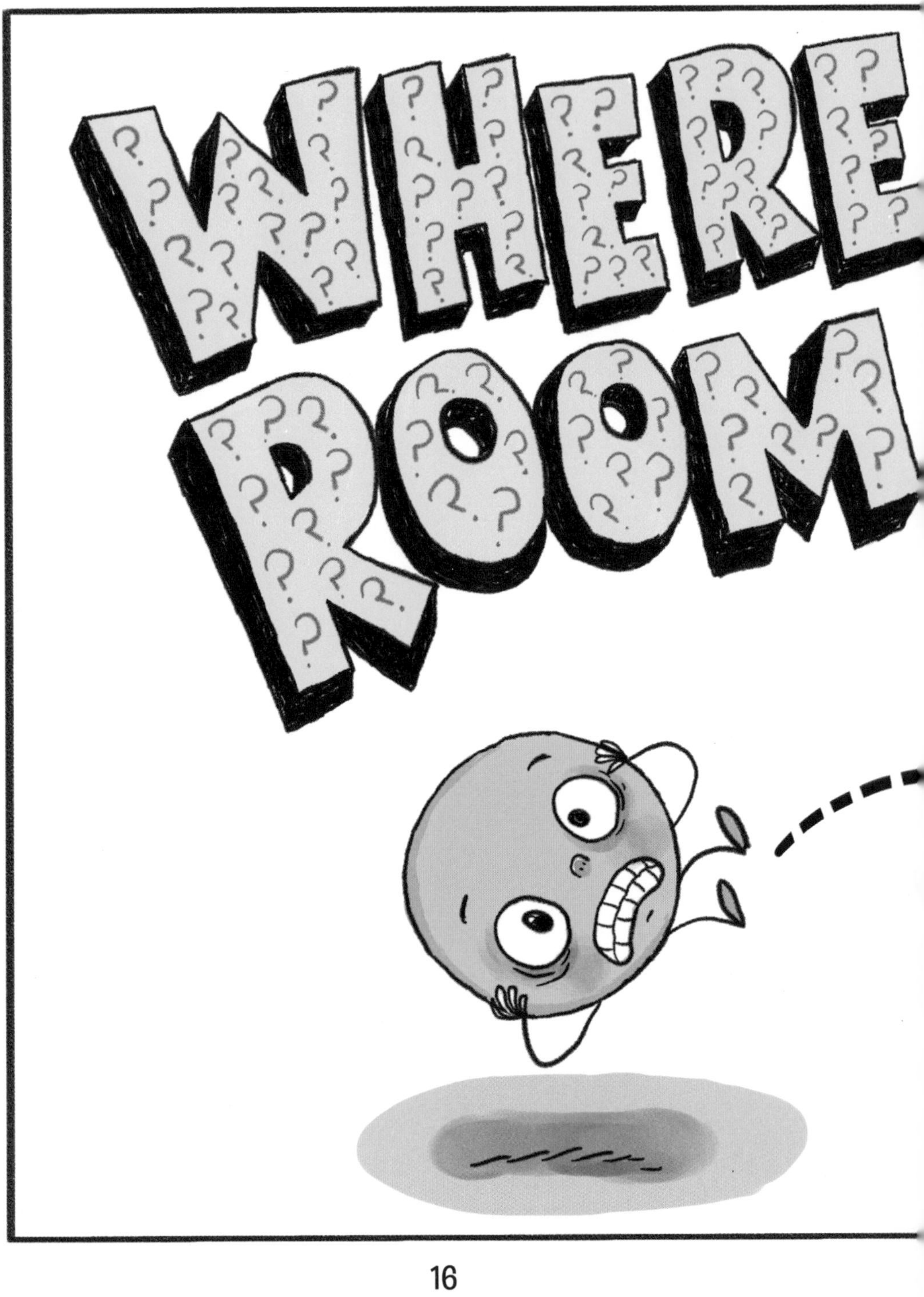
WHERE
ROOM

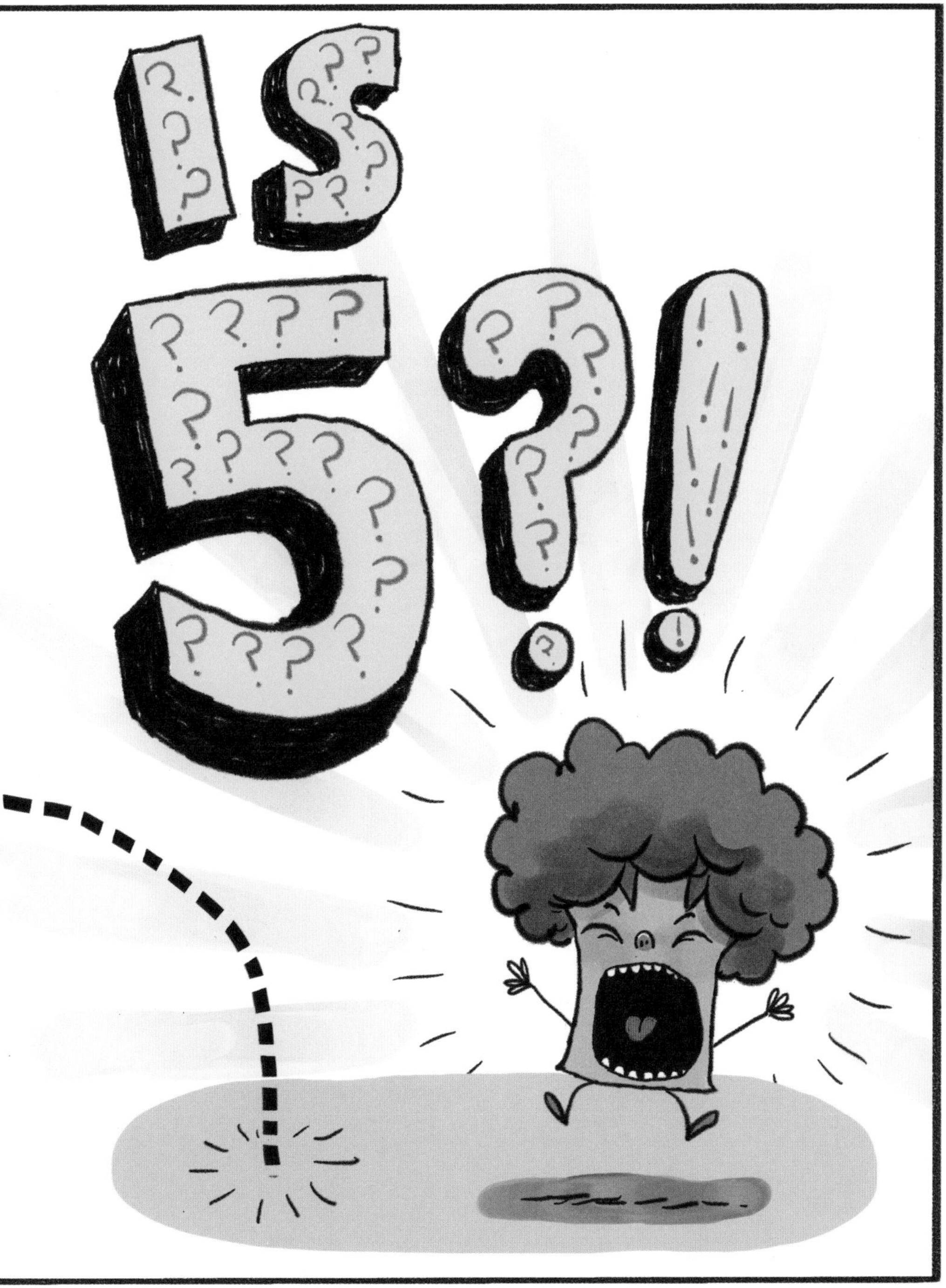
IS
5?!

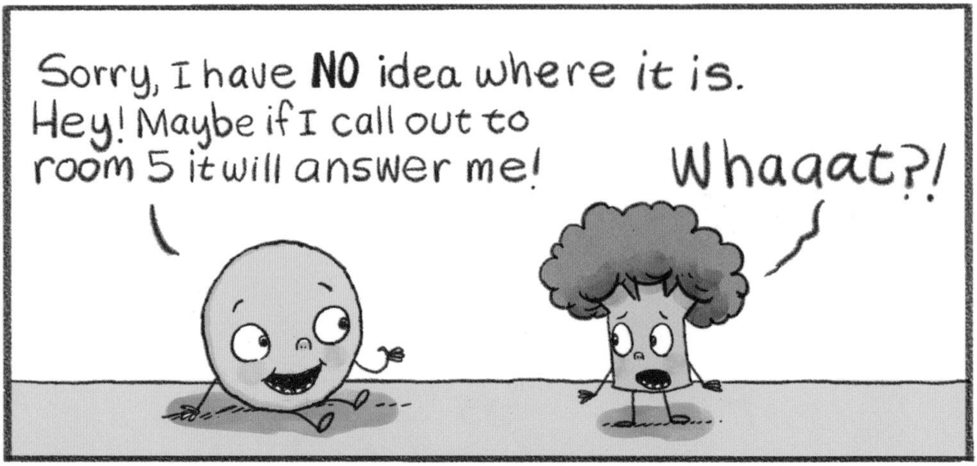
Sorry, I have NO idea where it is. Hey! Maybe if I call out to room 5 it will answer me!
Whaaat?!

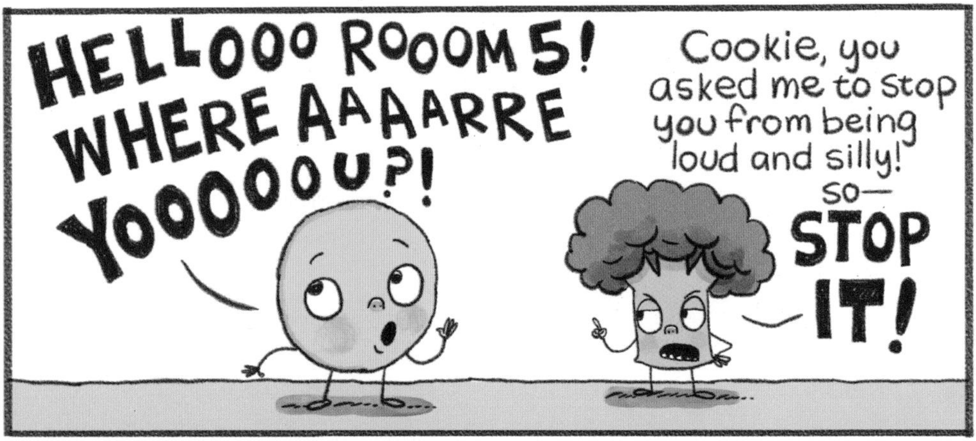
HELLOOO ROOOM 5! WHERE AAAARRE YOOOOOU?!
Cookie, you asked me to stop you from being loud and silly! SO—
STOP IT!

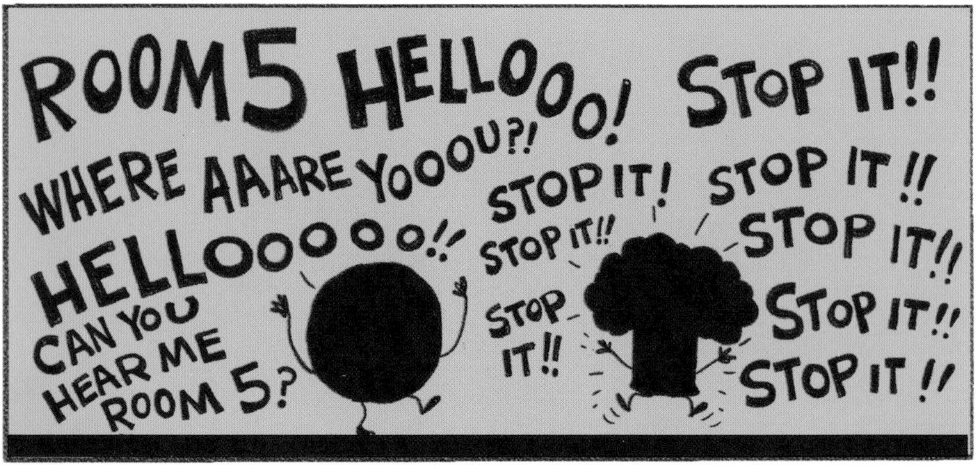
ROOM 5 HELLOOOO! WHERE AAARE YOOOU?!
HELLOOOOOO!!
CAN YOU HEAR ME ROOM 5?
STOP IT!!
STOP IT!
STOP IT!!
STOP IT!!
STOP IT!!
STOP IT!!
STOP IT!!
STOP IT!!
STOP IT!!

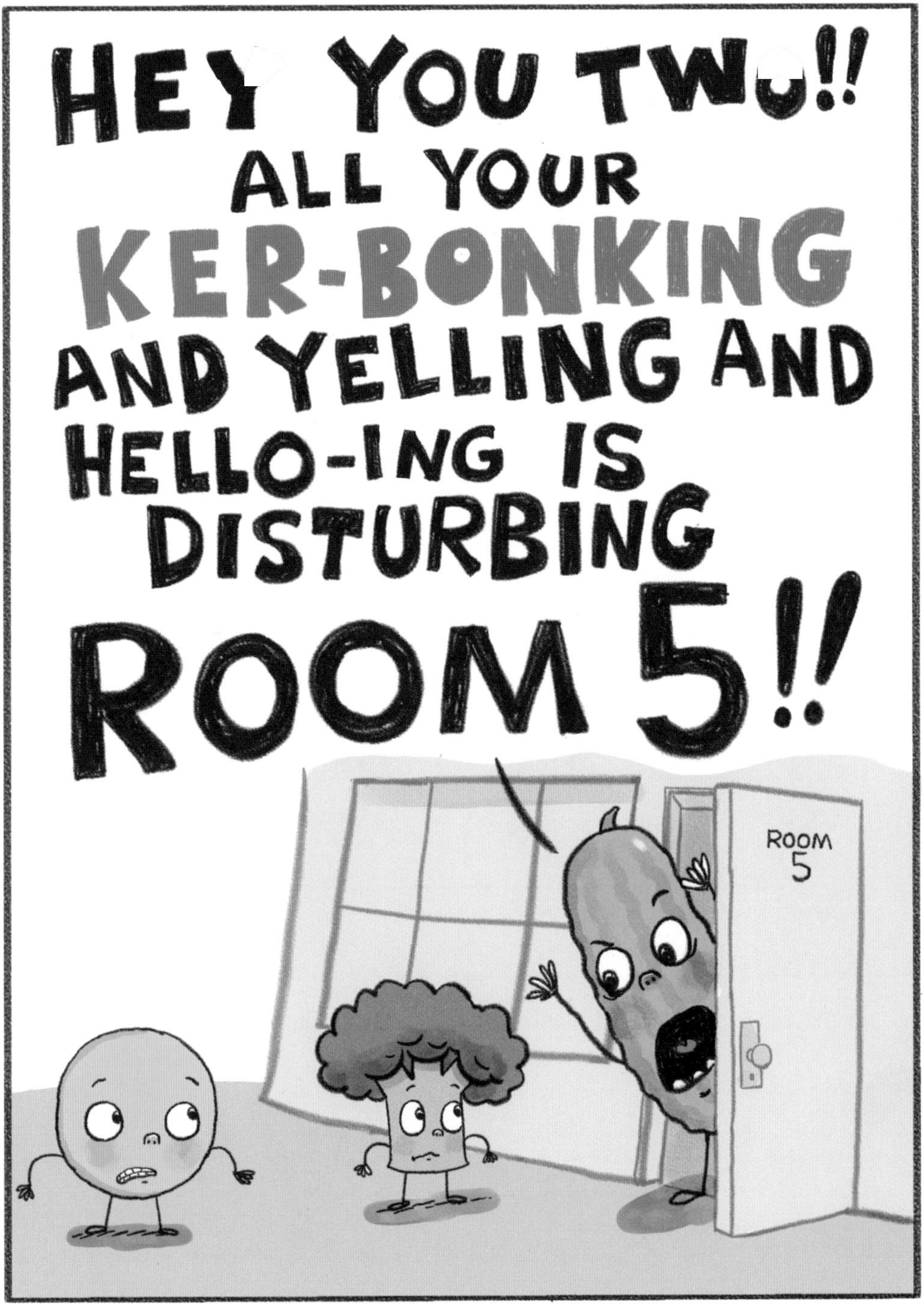
HEY YOU TWO!! ALL YOUR KER-BONKING AND YELLING AND HELLO-ING IS DISTURBING ROOM 5!!
ROOM 5

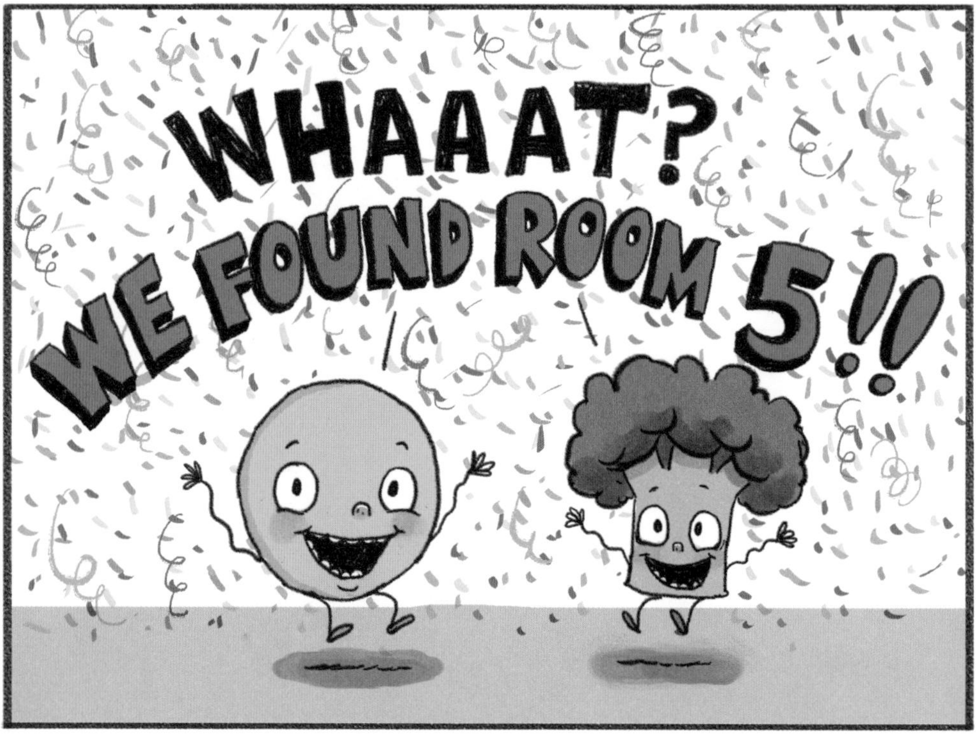
WHAAAT?
WE FOUND ROOM 5!!

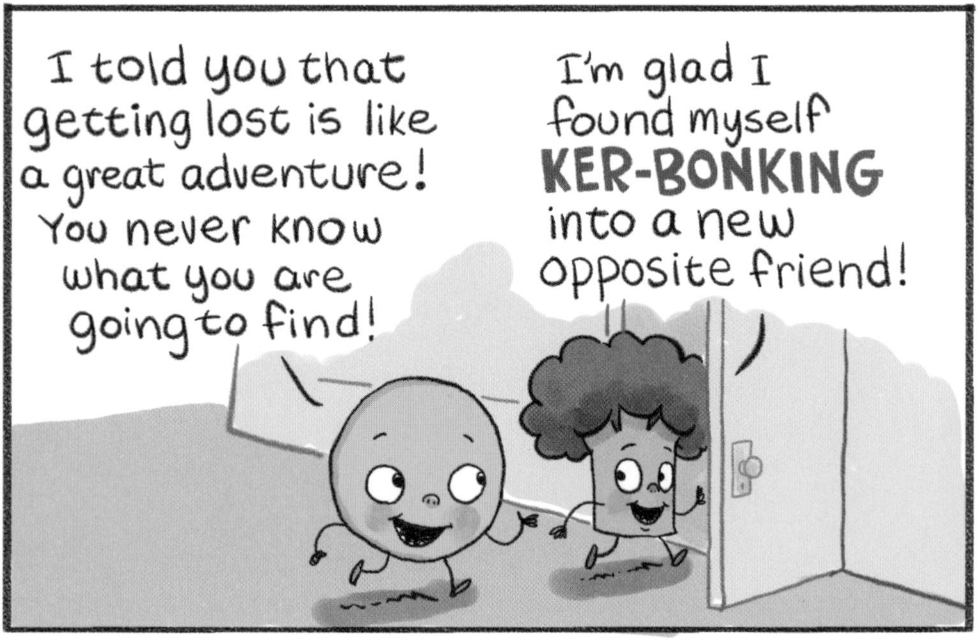
I told you that getting lost is like a great adventure! You never know what you are going to find!
I'm glad I found myself KER-BONKING into a new opposite friend!

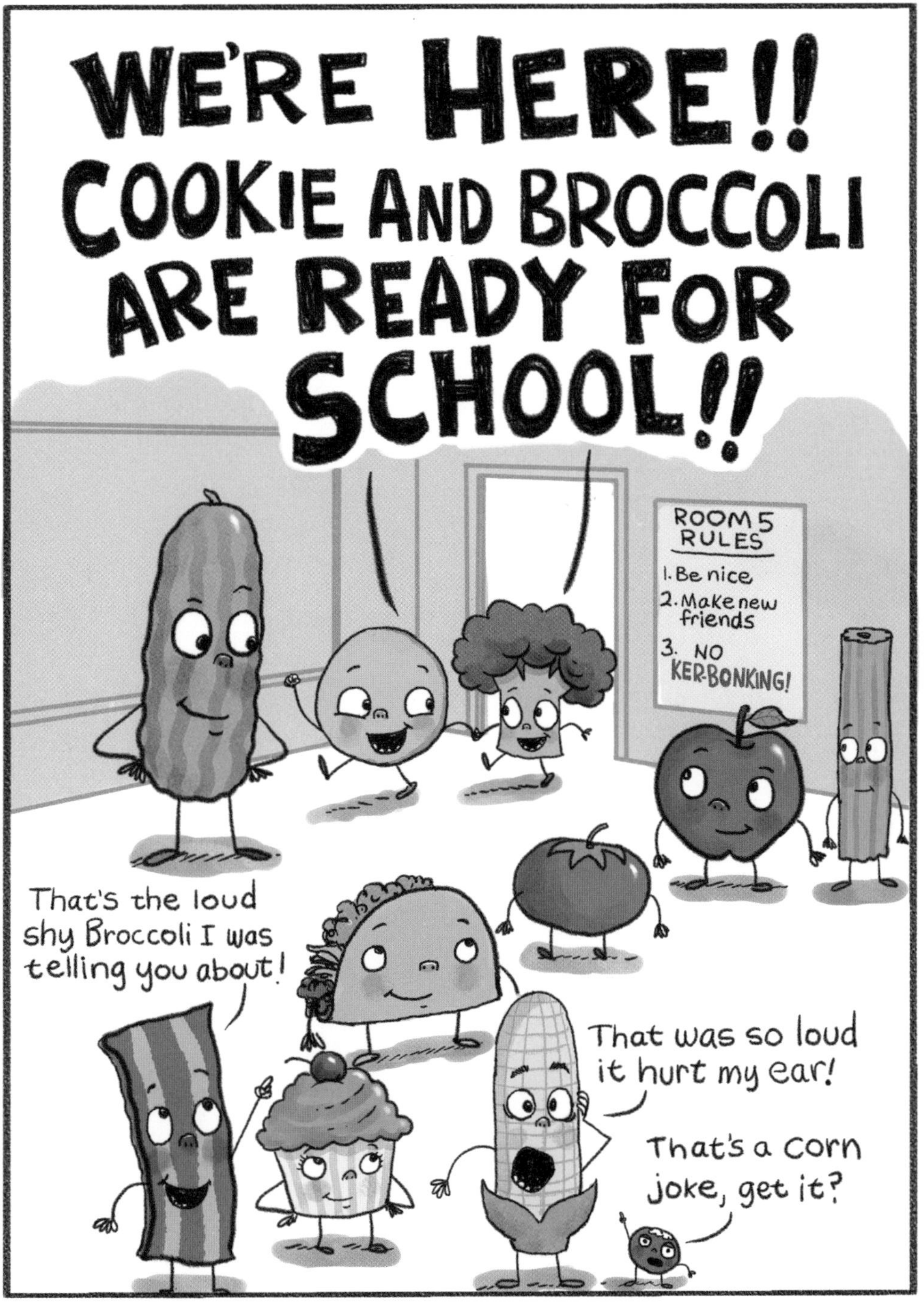

WE'RE HERE!! COOKIE AND BROCCOLI ARE READY FOR SCHOOL!!
ROOM 5 RULES
1. Be nice
2. Make new friends
3. NO KER-BONKING!
That's the loud shy Broccoli I was telling you about!
That was so loud it hurt my ear!
That's a corn joke, get it?

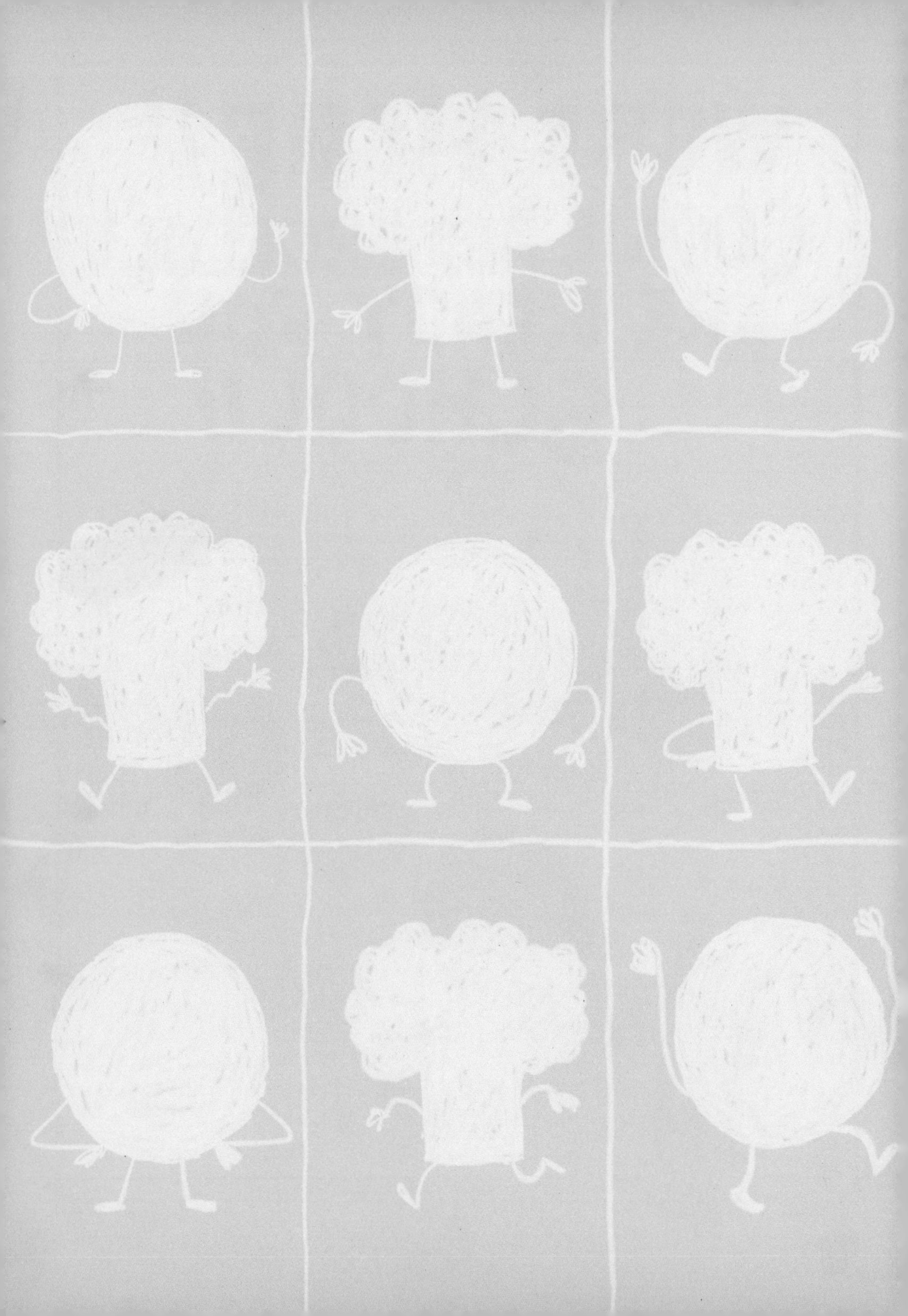

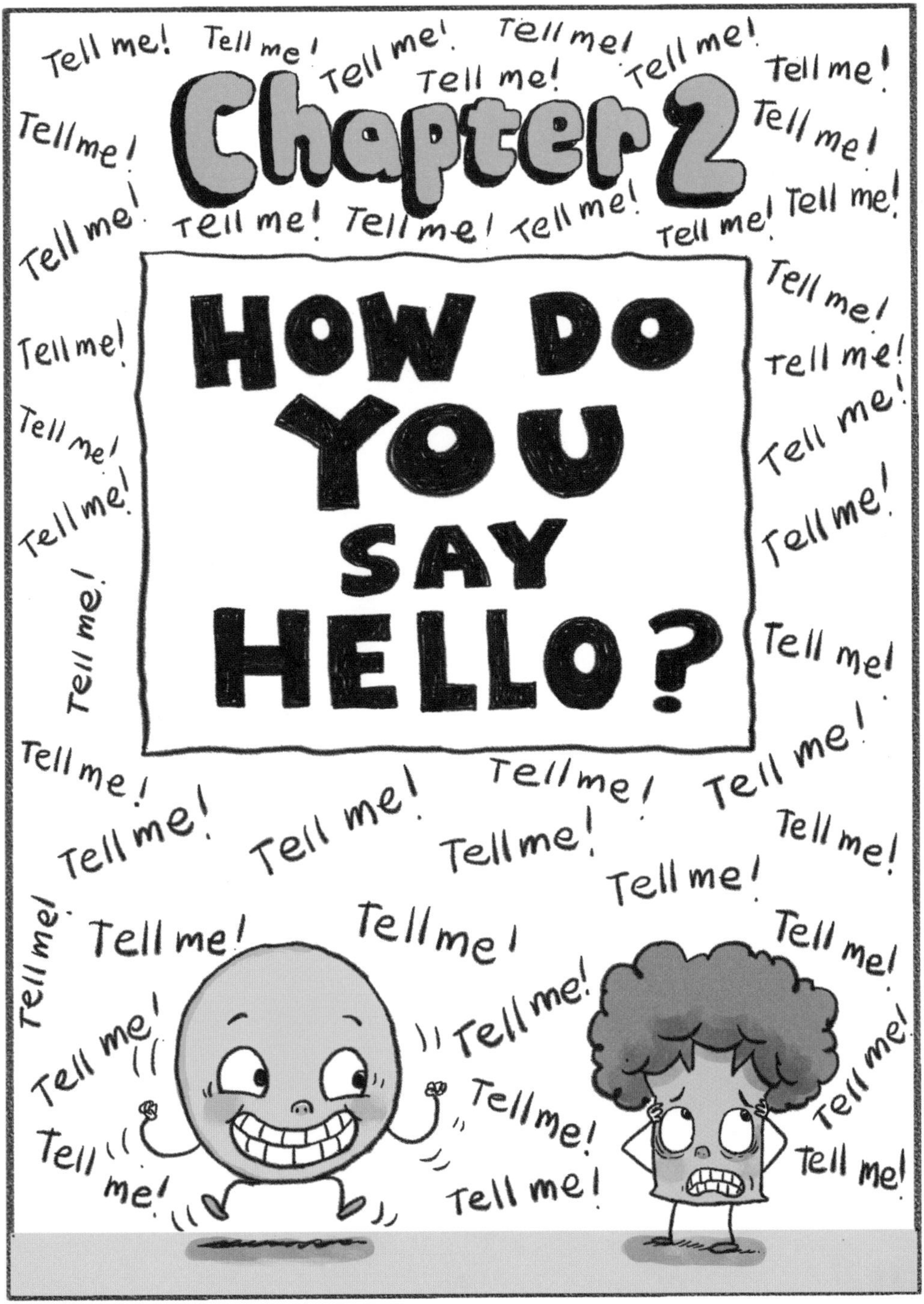

Chapter 2
HOW DO YOU SAY HELLO?
Tell me!
Tell me!
Tell me!
Tell me!
Tell me!
Tell me!
Tell me!
Tell me!
Tell me!
Tell me!
Tell me!
Tell me!
Tell me!
Tell me!
Tell me!
Tell me!
Tell me!
Tell me!
Tell me!
Tell me!
Tell me!
Tell me!
Tell me!
Tell me!
Tell me!
Tell me!
Tell me!
Tell me!
Tell me!
Tell me!
Tell me!
Tell me!
Tell me!
Tell me!
Tell me!
Tell me!
Tell me!
Tell me!
Tell me!
Tell me!
Tell me!
Tell me!
Tell me!

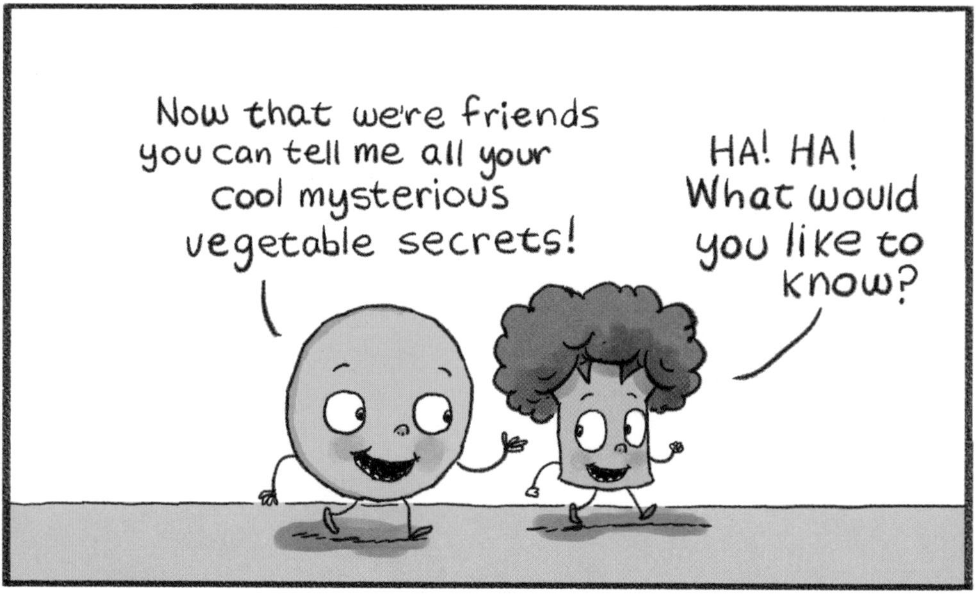
Now that were friends you can tell me all your cool mysterious vegetable secrets!
HA! HA! What would you like to know?

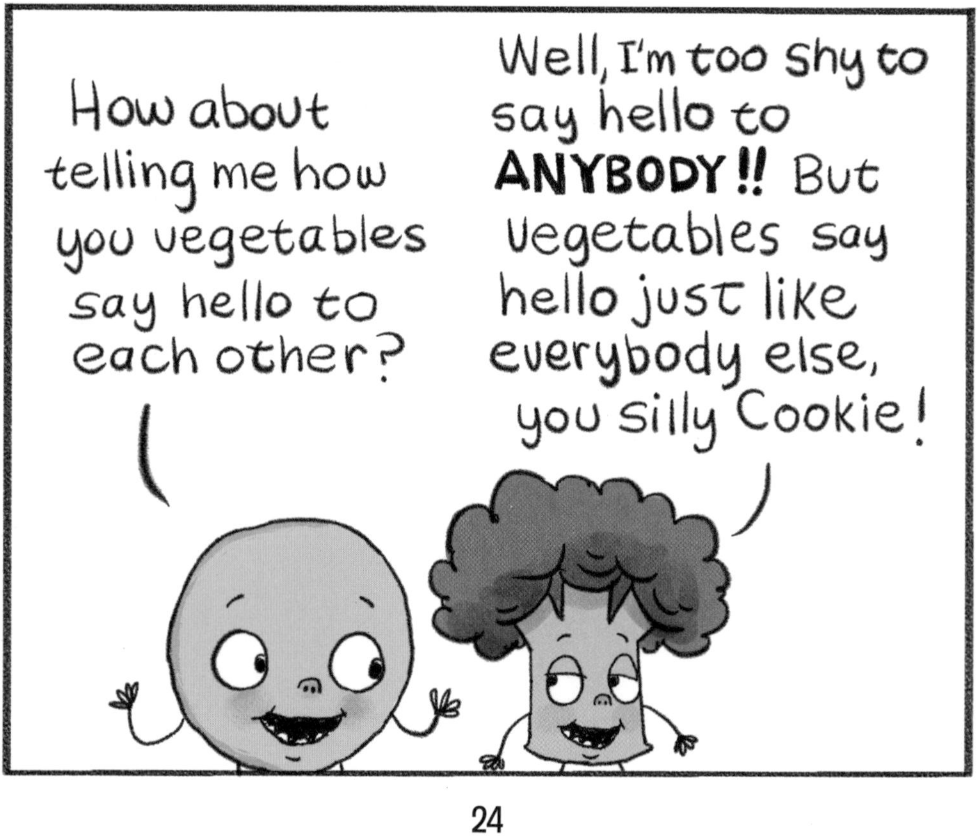
How about telling me how you vegetables say hello to each other?
Well, I'm too shy to say hello to ANYBODY!! But Vegetables say hello just like everybody else, you silly Cookie!

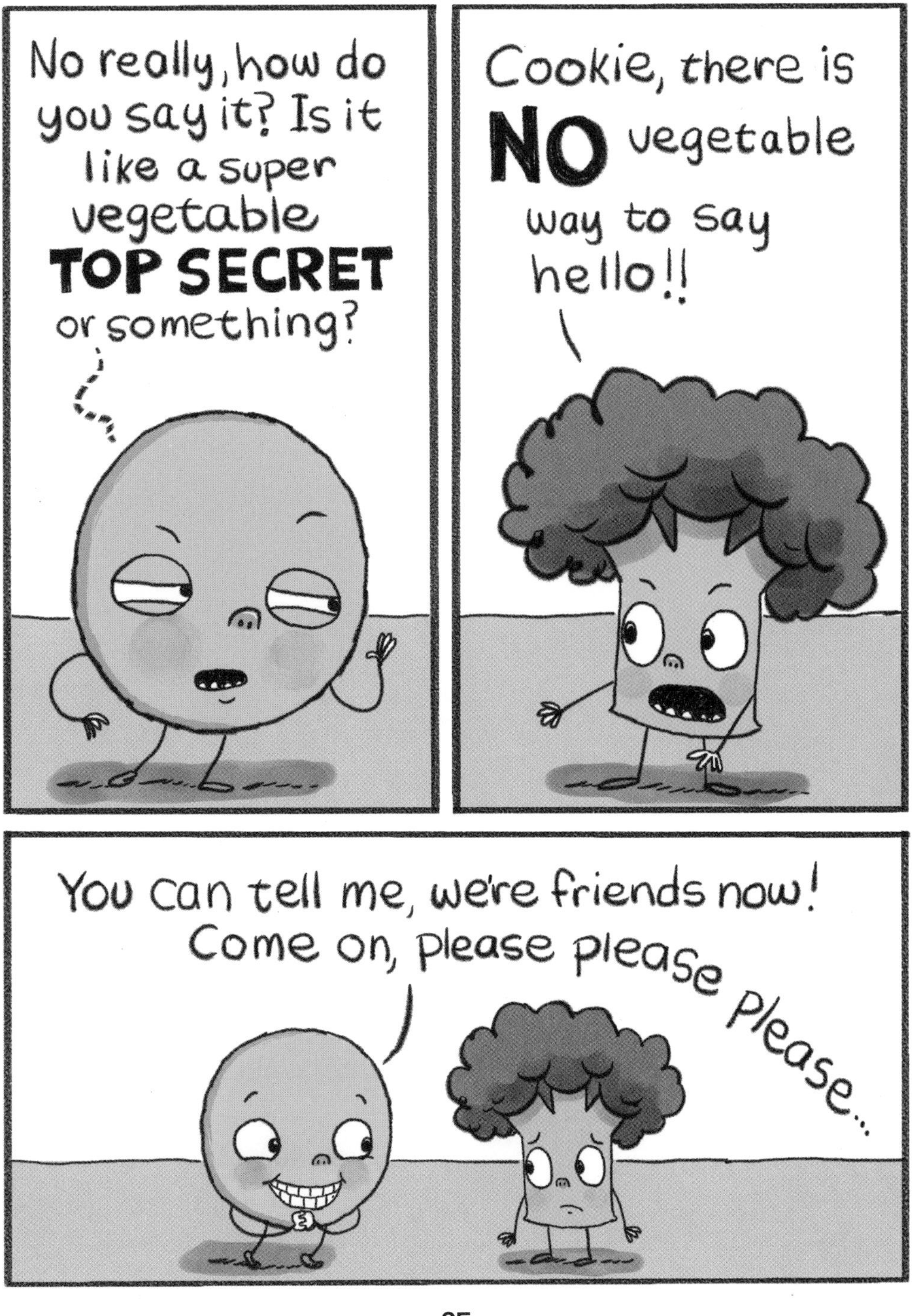
No really, how do you say it? Is it like a super vegetable TOP SECRET or something?
Cookie, there is NO vegetable way to say hello!!
You can tell me, we're friends now! Come on, please please please please...

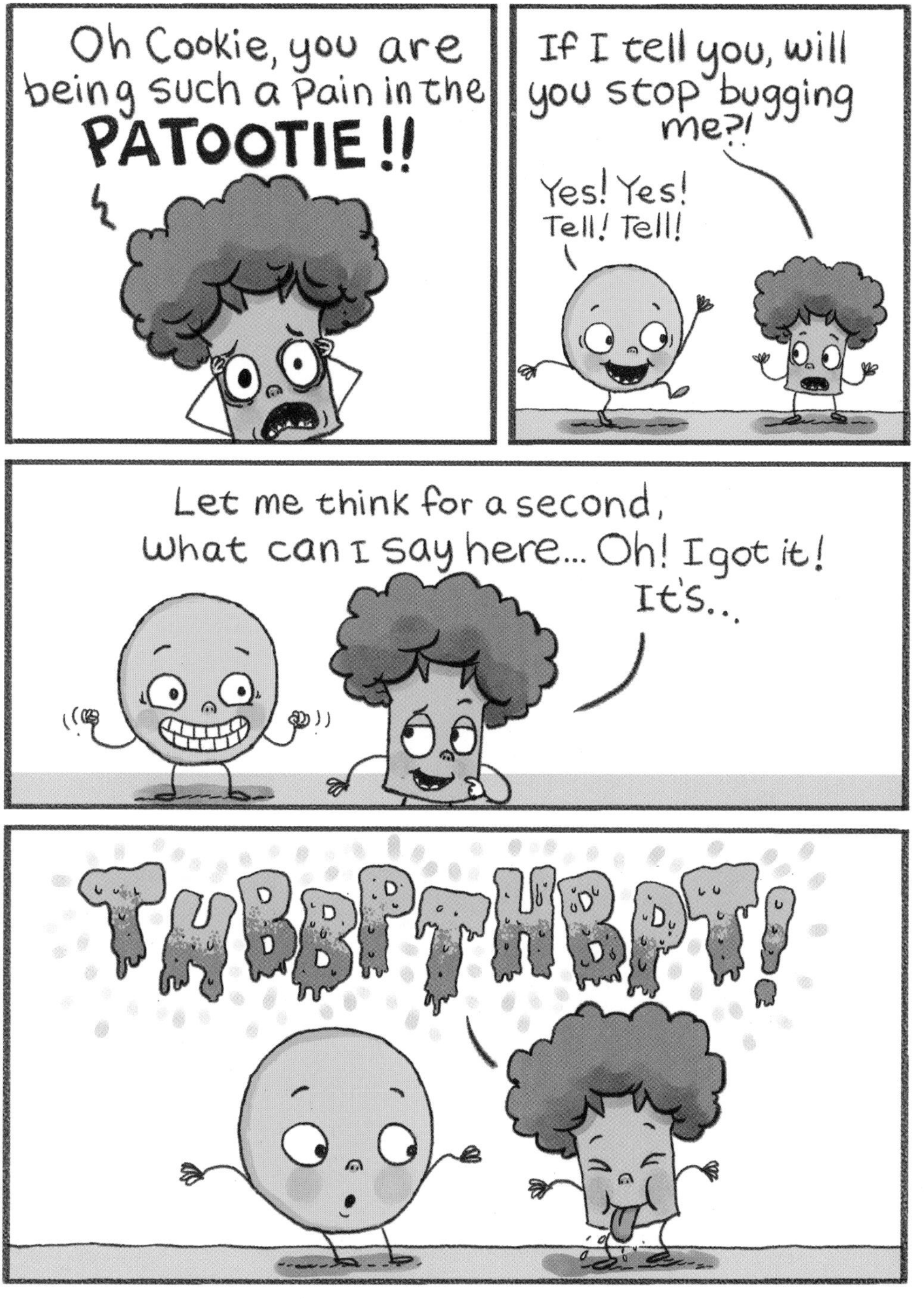
Oh Cookie, you are being such a Pain in the PATOOTIE !!
If I tell you, will you stop bugging me?!
Yes! Yes! Tell! Tell!
Let me think for a second, what can I say here... Oh! I got it! It's...
THBPTHBPT!

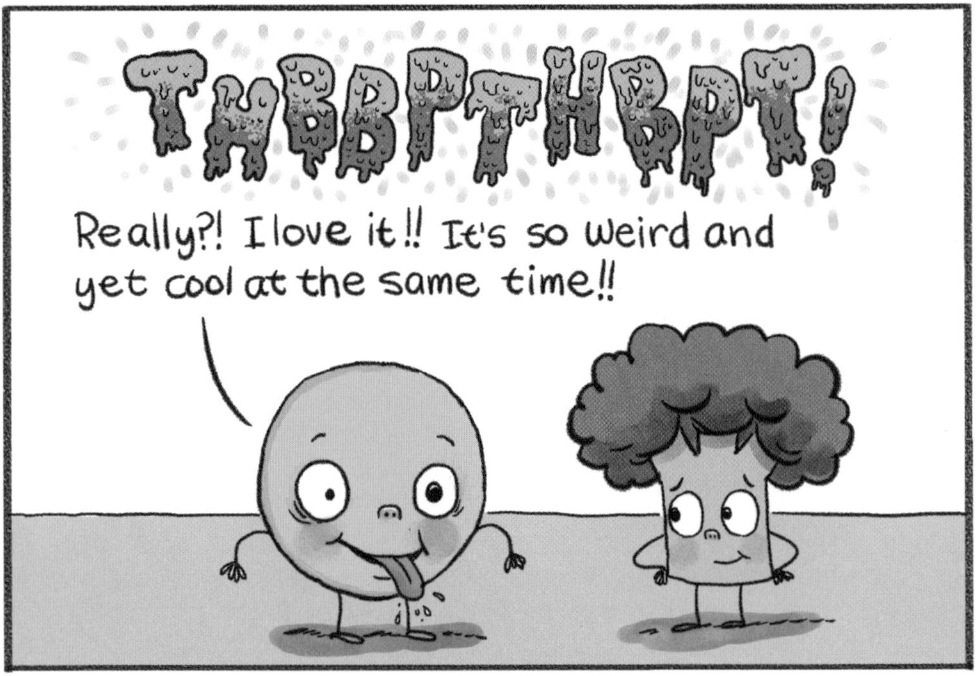
THBBPTHBPT!
Really?! I love it!! It's so weird and yet cool at the same time!!

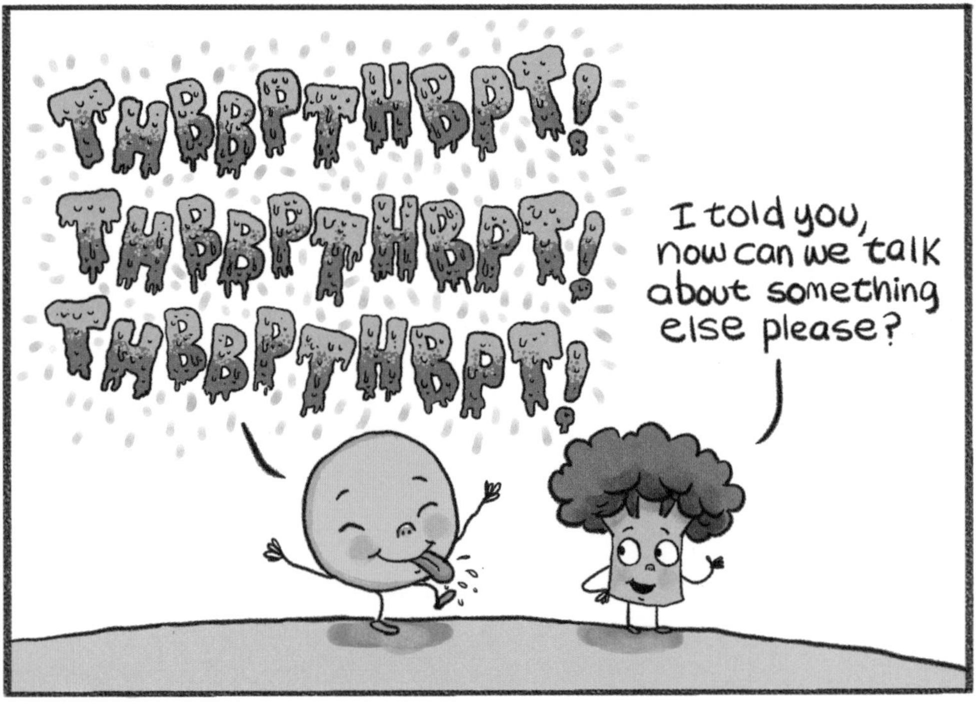
THBBPTHBPT!
THBBPTHBPT!
THBBPTHBPT!
I told you, now can we talk about something else please?

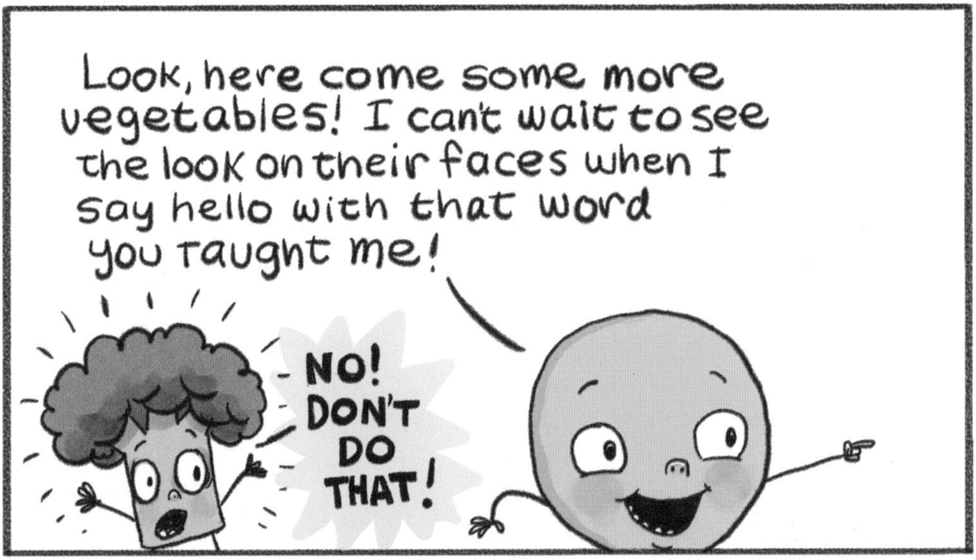
Look, here come some more vegetables! I can't wait to see the look on their faces when I say hello with that word you taught me!
NO! DON'T DO THAT!

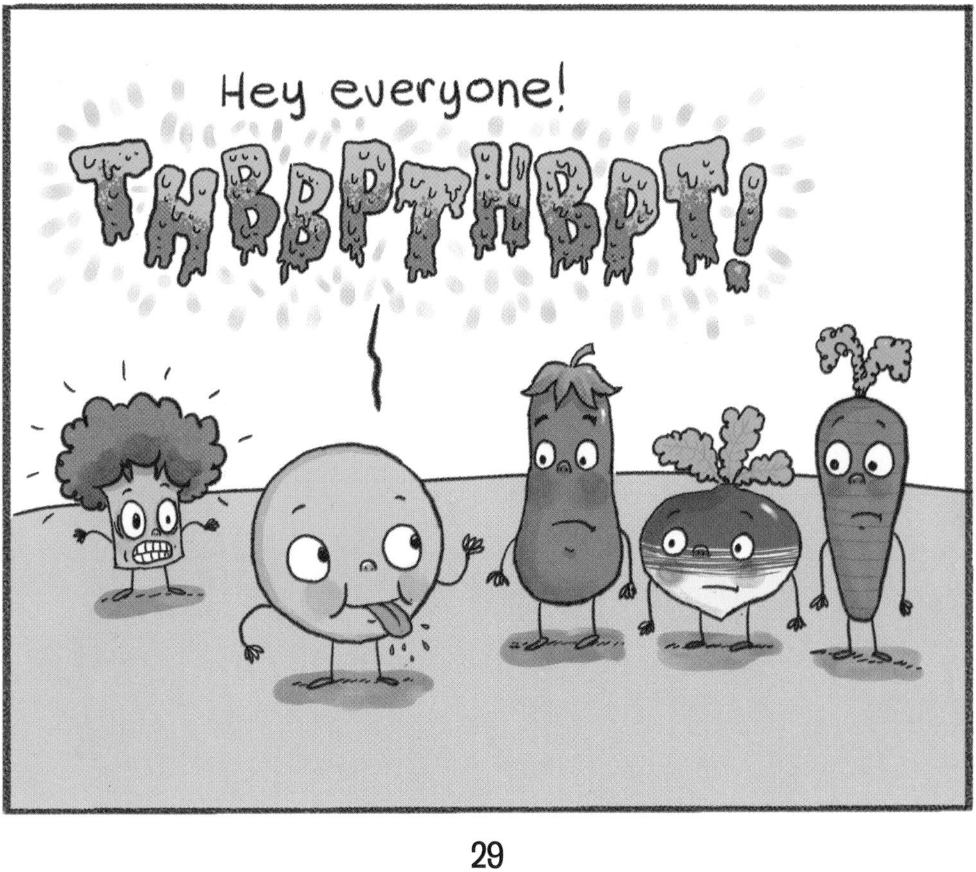
Hey everyone!
THBBPTHBPT!

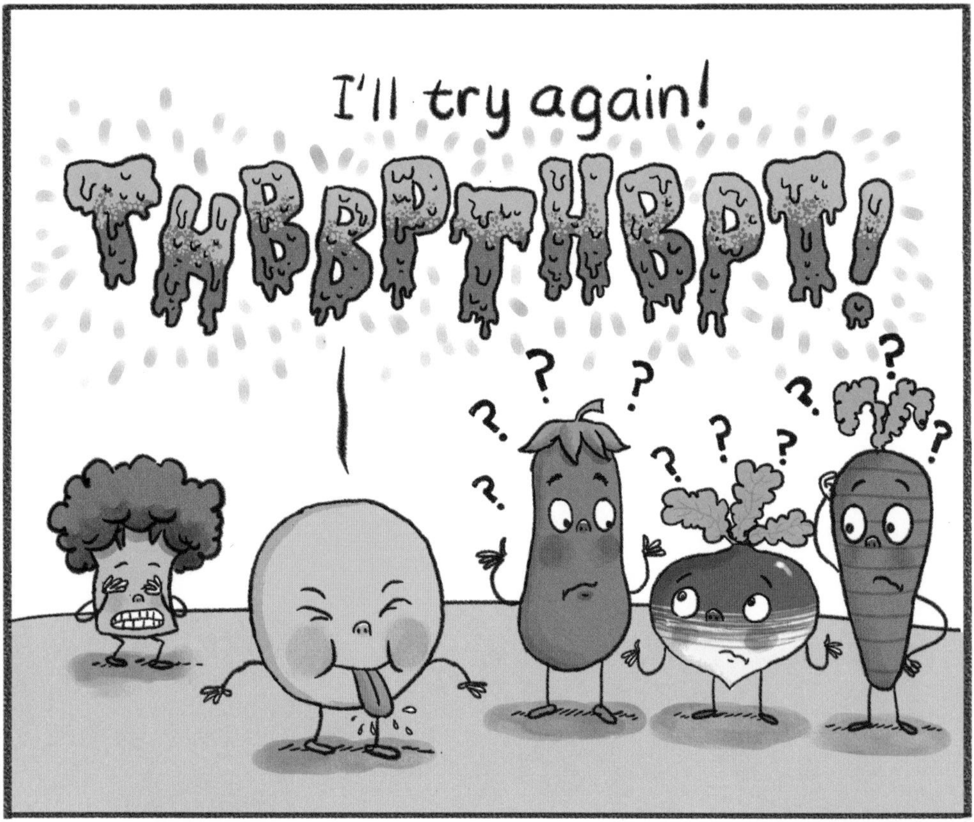
I'll try again!
THBBPTHBPT!

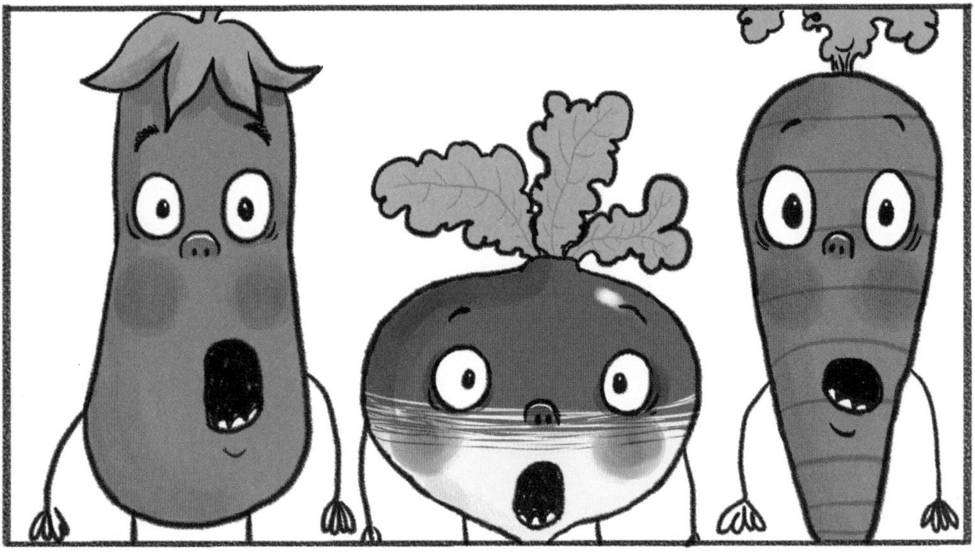

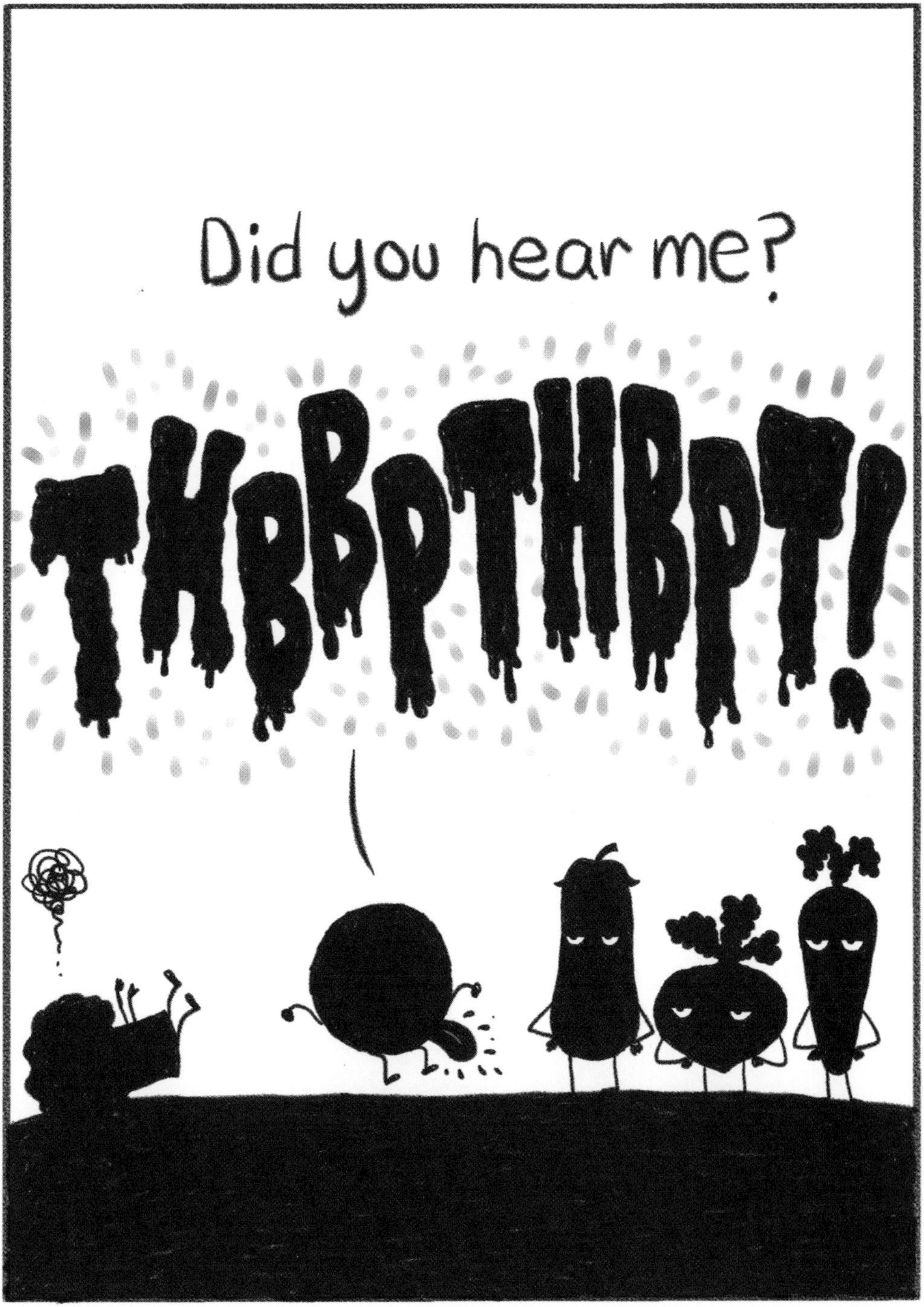
Did you hear me?
THBBPTHBPT!

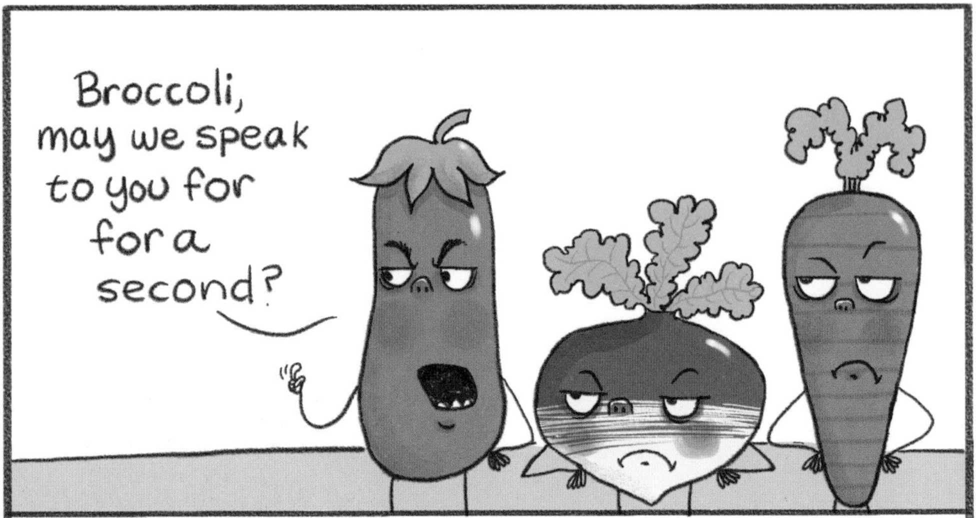
Broccoli, may we speak to you for for a second?

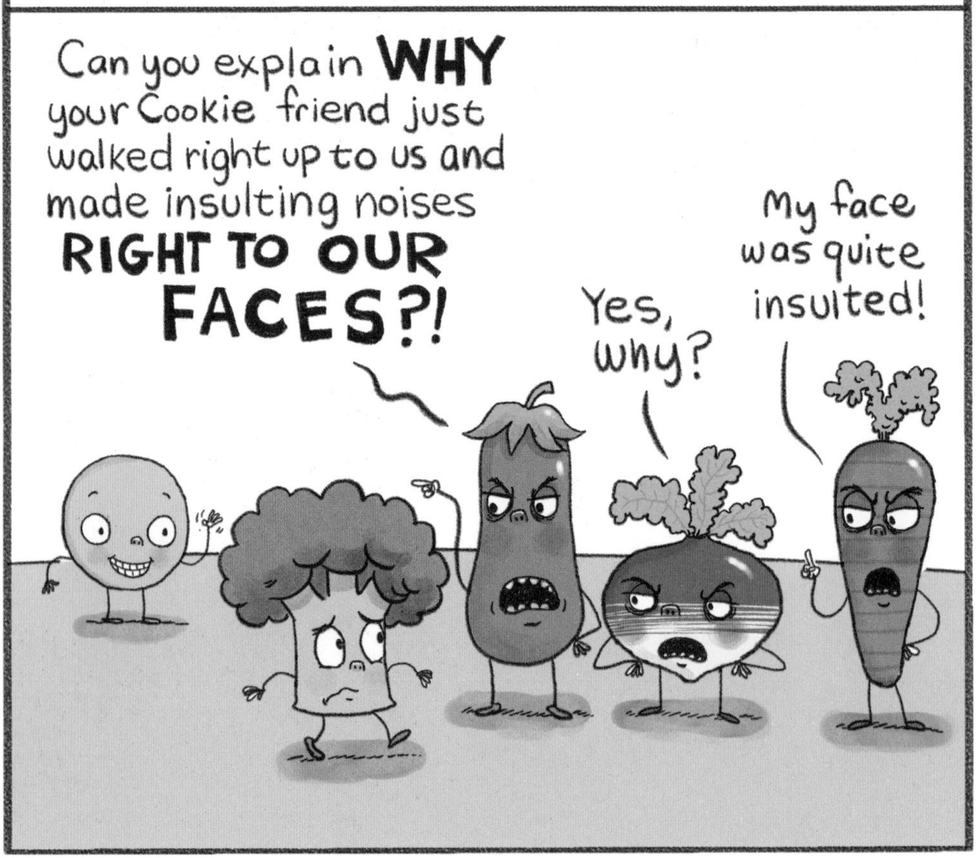
Can you explain WHY your Cookie friend just walked right up to us and made insulting noises RIGHT TO OUR FACES?!
Yes, why?
My face was quite insulted!

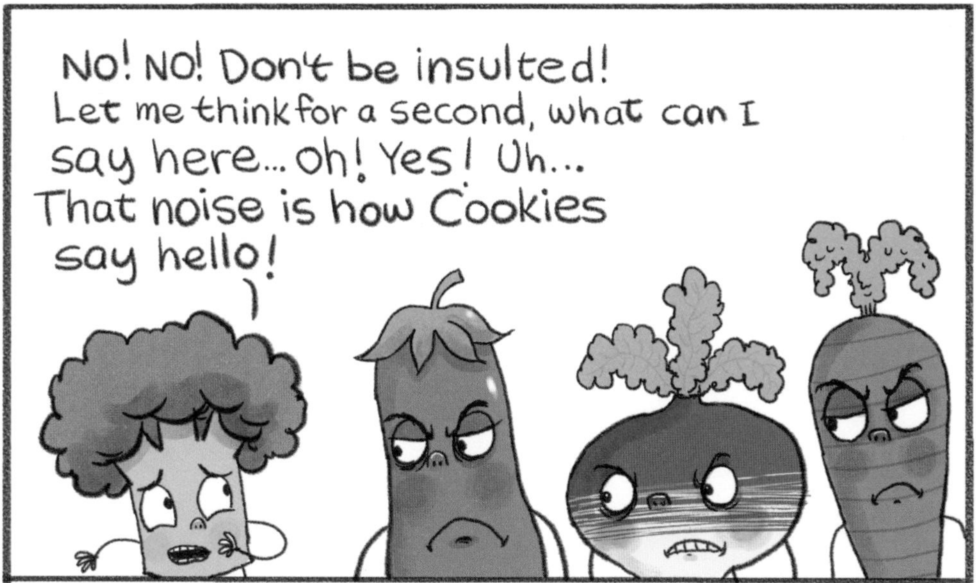
NO! NO! Don't be insulted! Let me think for a second, what can I say here... Oh! Yes! Uh... That noise is how Cookies say hello!

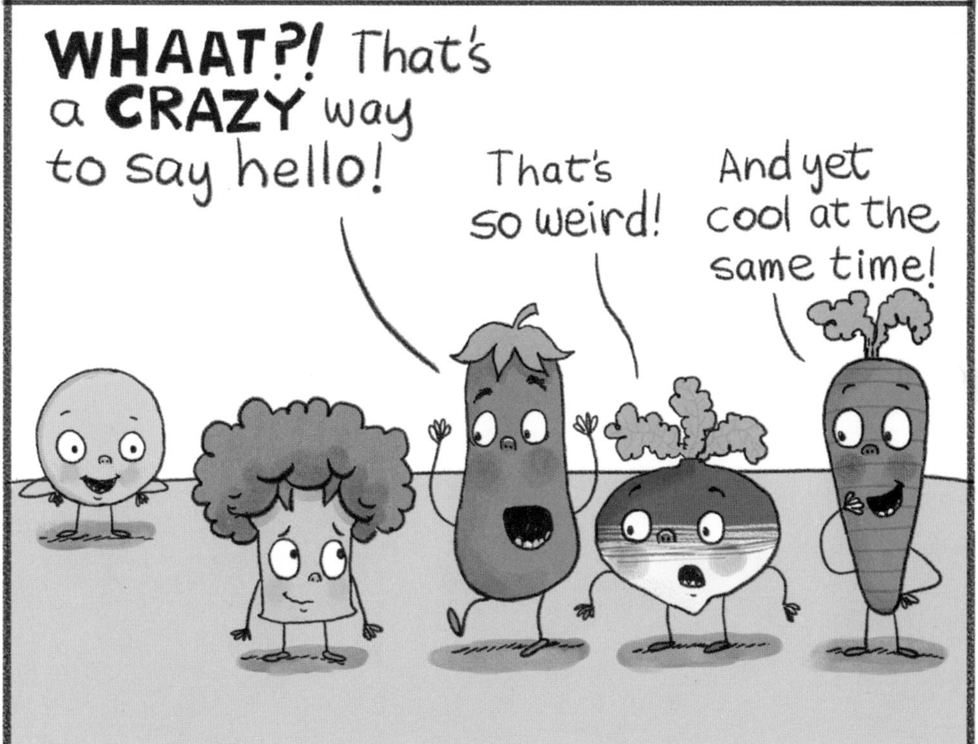
WHAAT?! That's a **CRAZY** way to say hello!
That's so weird!
And yet cool at the same time!

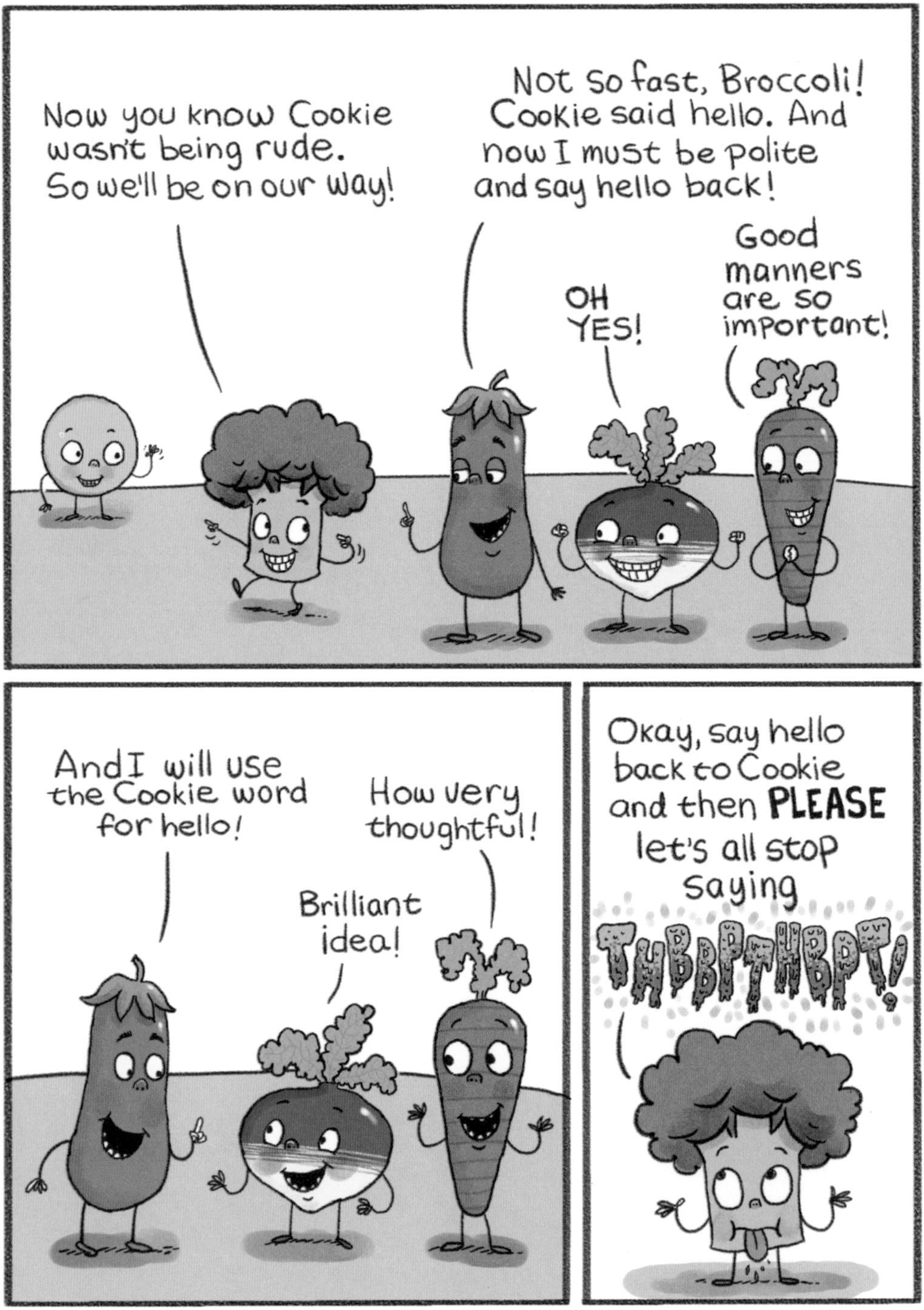
Now you know Cookie wasn't being rude. So we'll be on our way!
Not so fast, Broccoli! Cookie said hello. And now I must be polite and say hello back!
OH YES!
Good manners are so important!
And I will use the Cookie word for hello!
Brilliant idea!
How very thoughtful!
Okay, say hello back to Cookie and then **PLEASE** let's all stop saying
THBBPTHBPT!

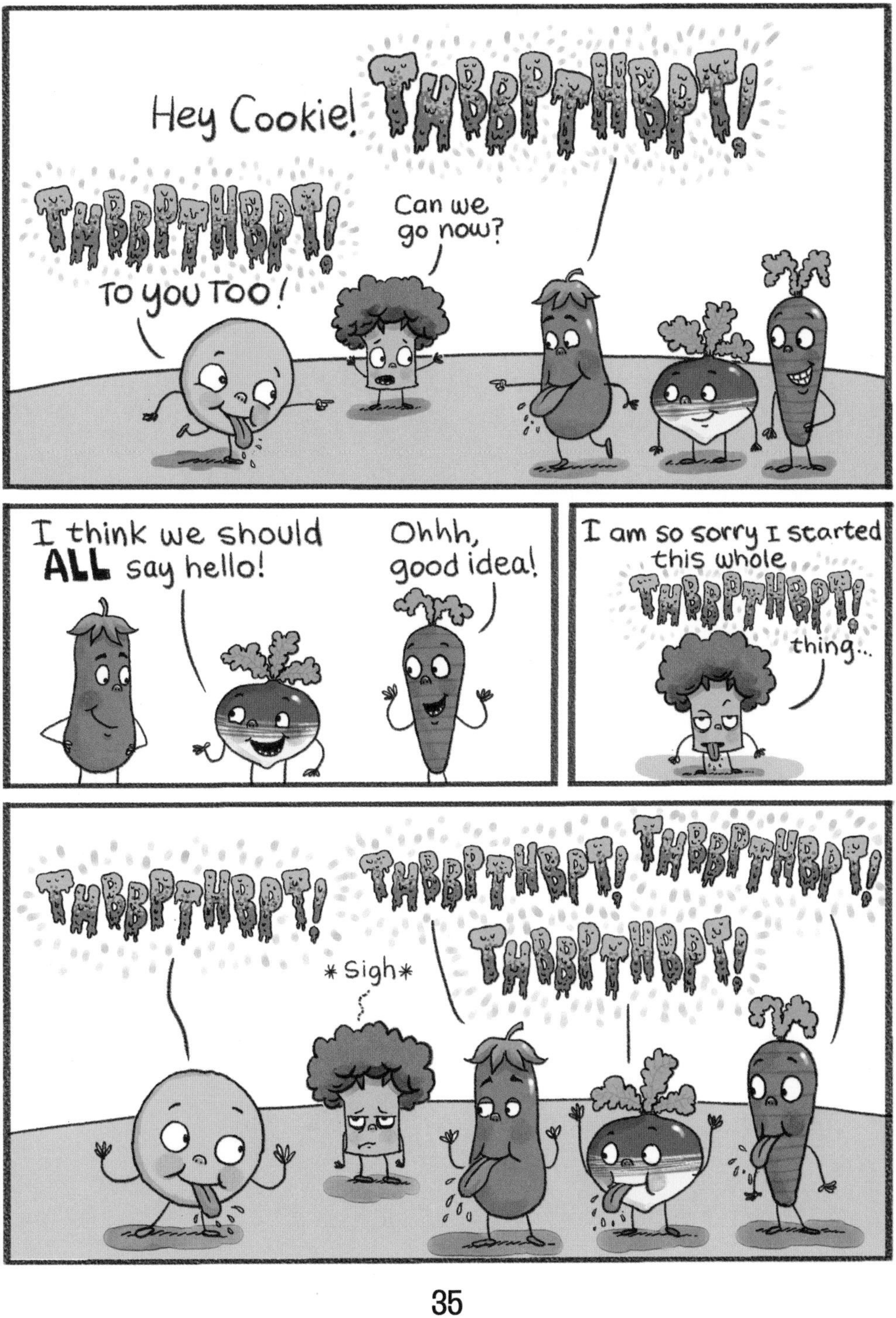

Hey Cookie! THBBPTHBPT!
THBBPTHBPT! TO YOU TOO!
Can we go now?
I think we should ALL say hello!
Ohhh, good idea!
I am so sorry I started this whole THBBPTHBPT! thing...
THBBPTHBPT!
Sigh
THBBPTHBPT!
THBBPTHBPT!
THBBPTHBPT!

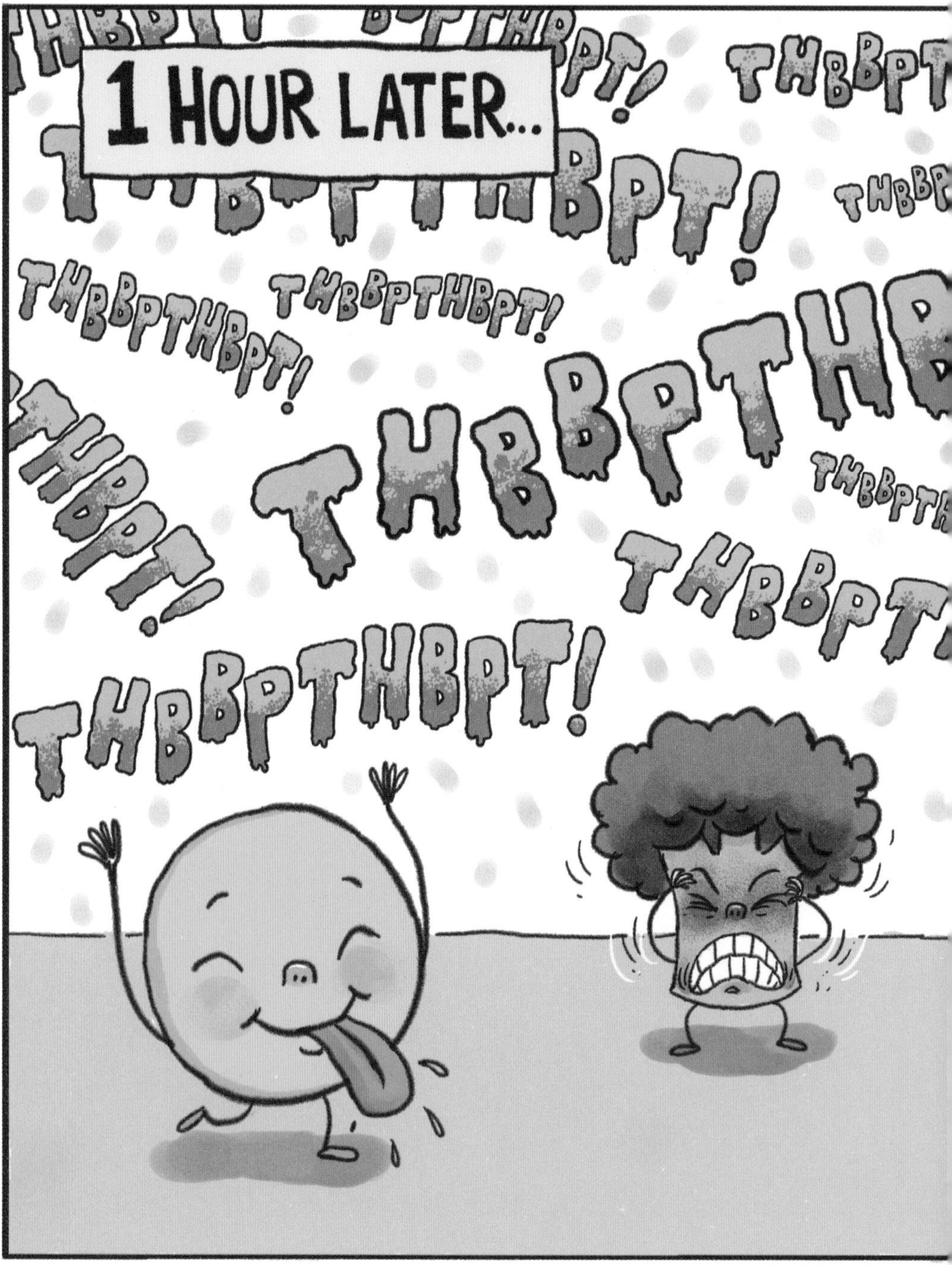
1 HOUR LATER...
THBPTHBPT!
THBPTHBPT!
THBPTHBPT!
THBPT!
THBPTHBPT!

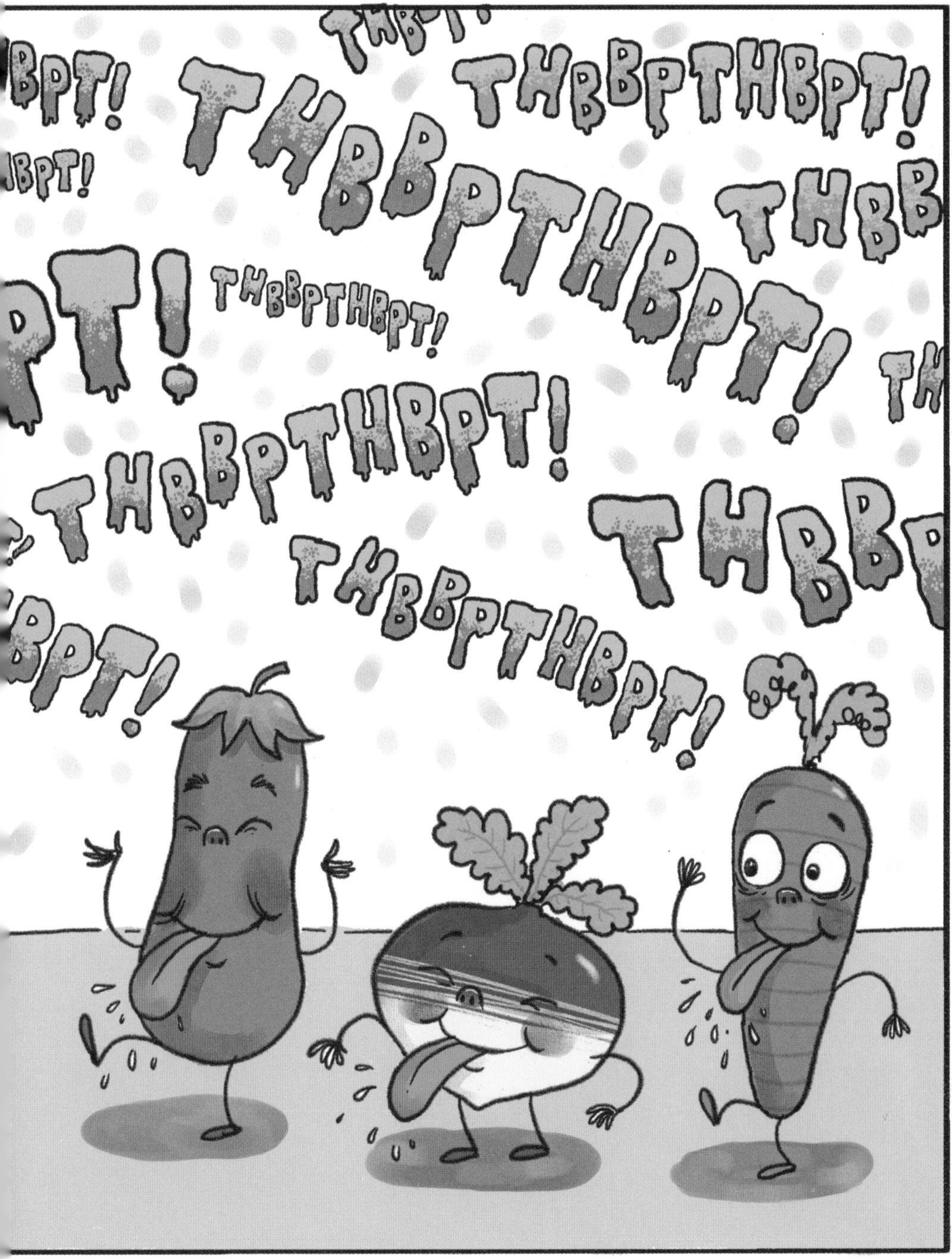
THBBPTHBPT!
THBBPTHBPT!
THBBPTHBPT!
THBBPTHBPT!
THBBPTHBPT!

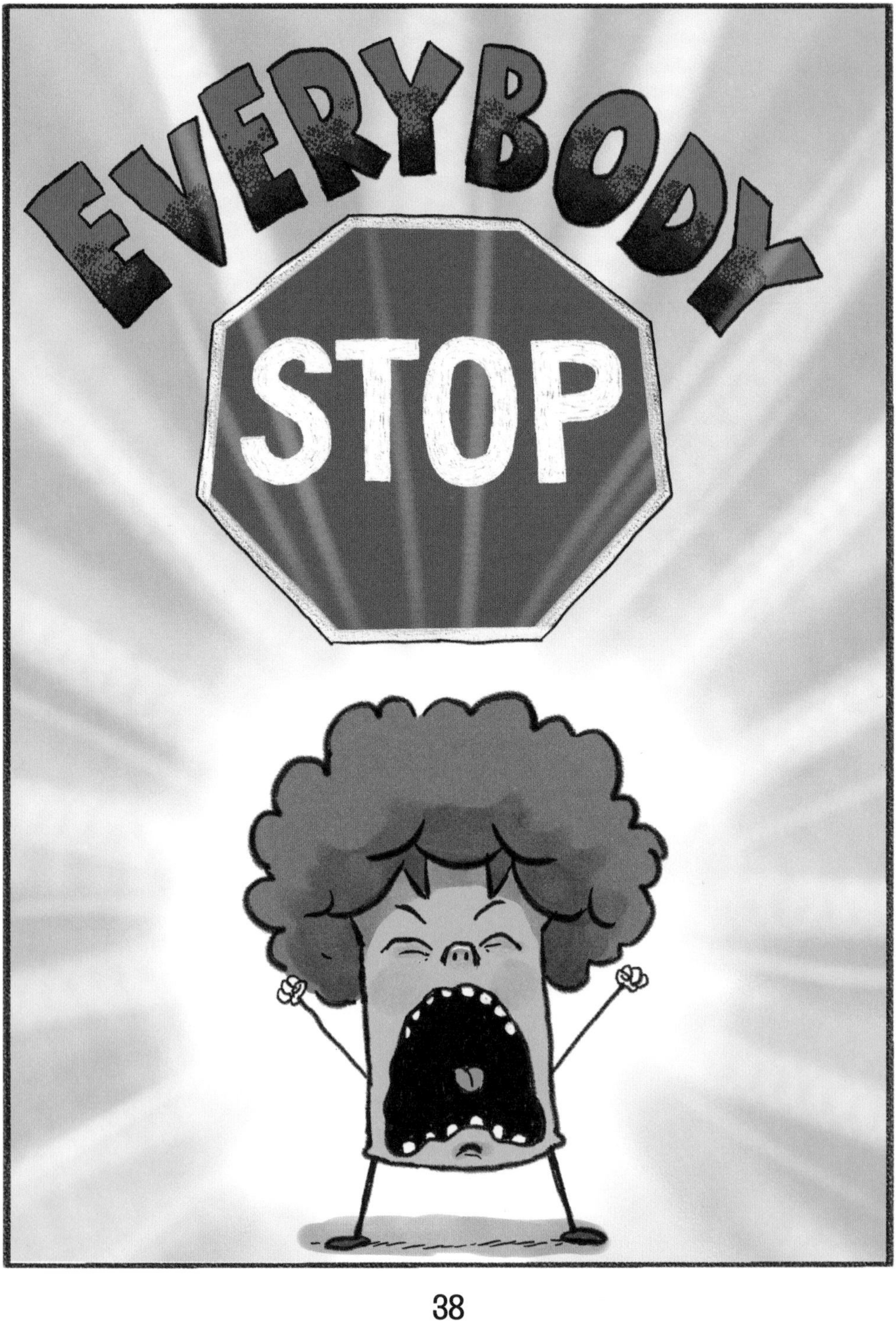
EVERYBODY
STOP

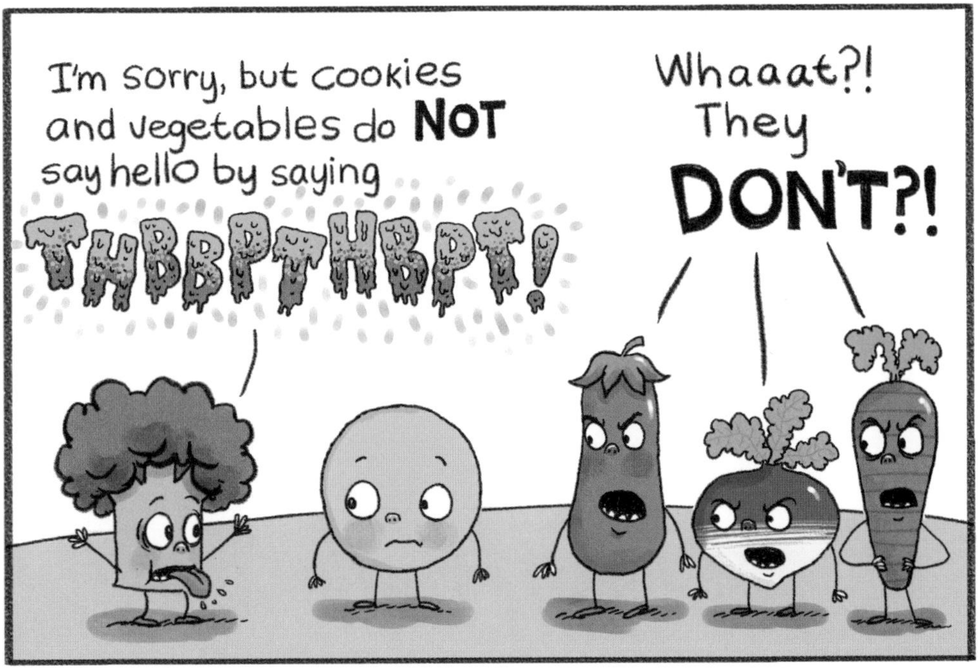
I'm sorry, but cookies and vegetables do NOT say hello by saying
THBBPTHBPT!
Whaaat?! They DON'T?!

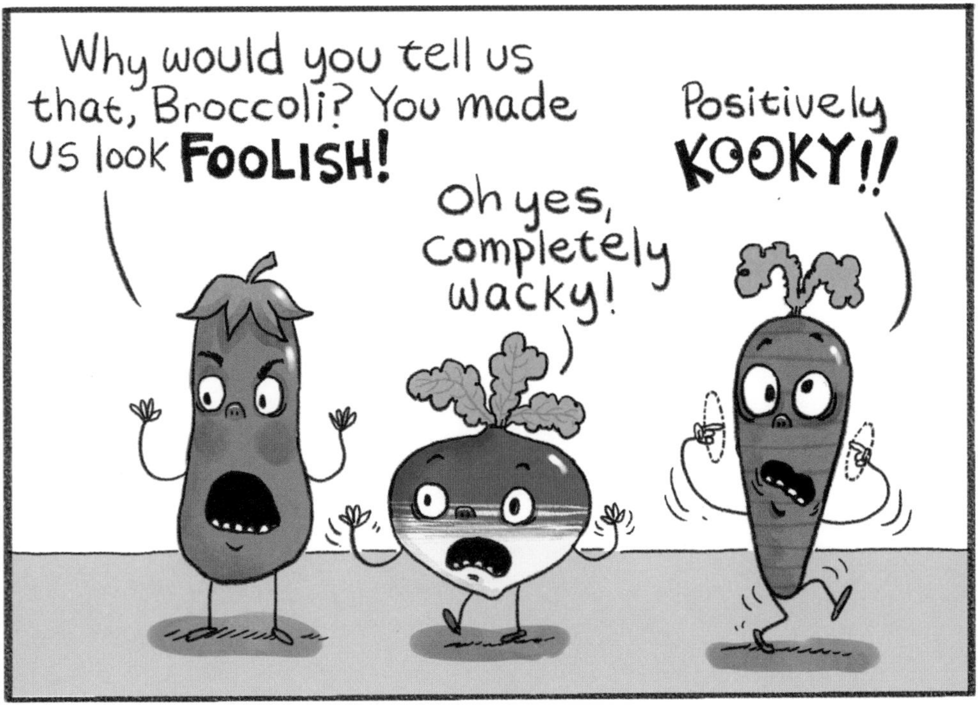
Why would you tell us that, Broccoli? You made us look FOOLISH!
Oh yes, completely wacky!
Positively KOOKY!!

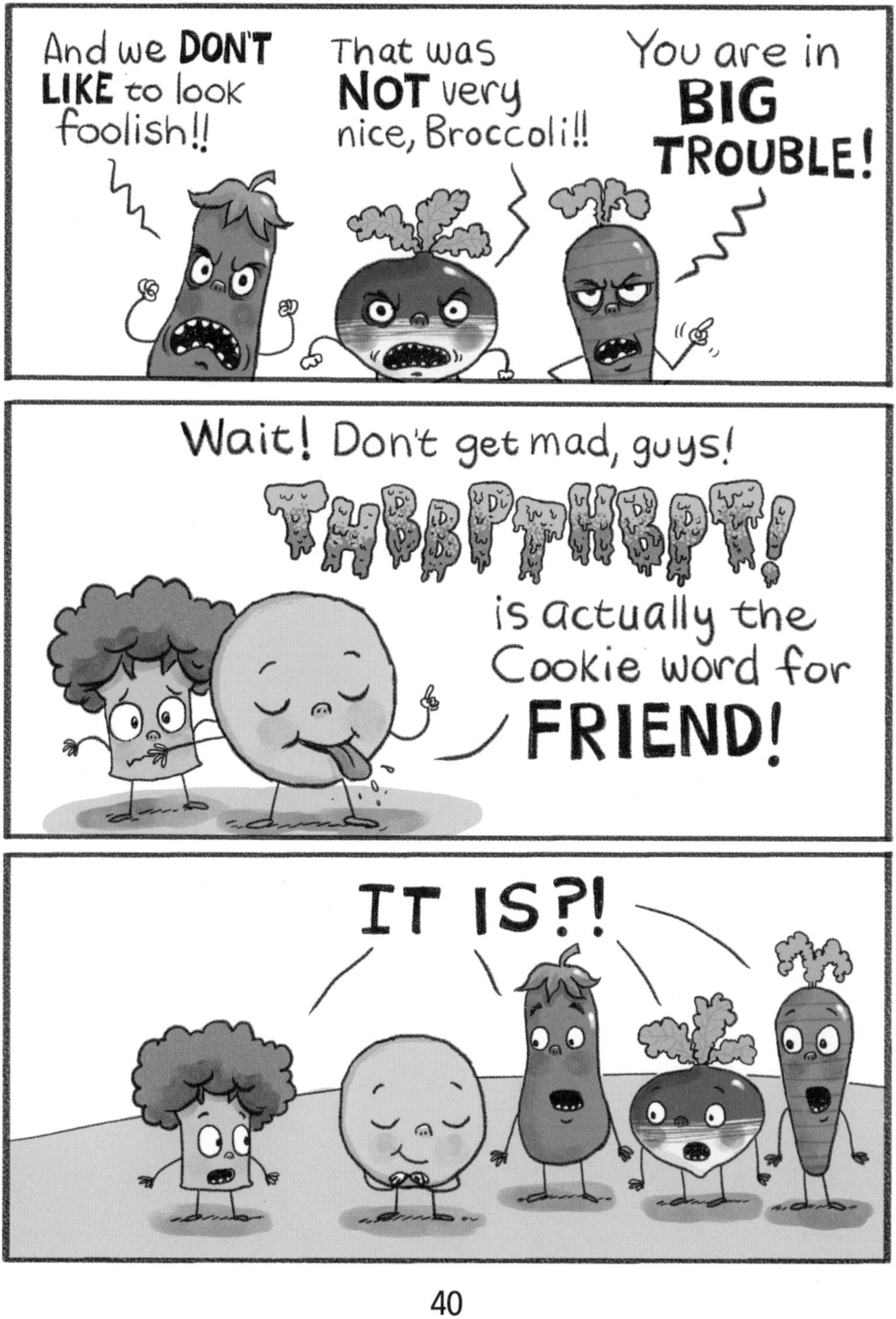
And we DON'T LIKE to look foolish!!
That was NOT very nice, Broccoli!!
You are in BIG TROUBLE!
Wait! Don't get mad, guys!
THBBPTHBPT!
is actually the Cookie word for FRIEND!
IT IS?!

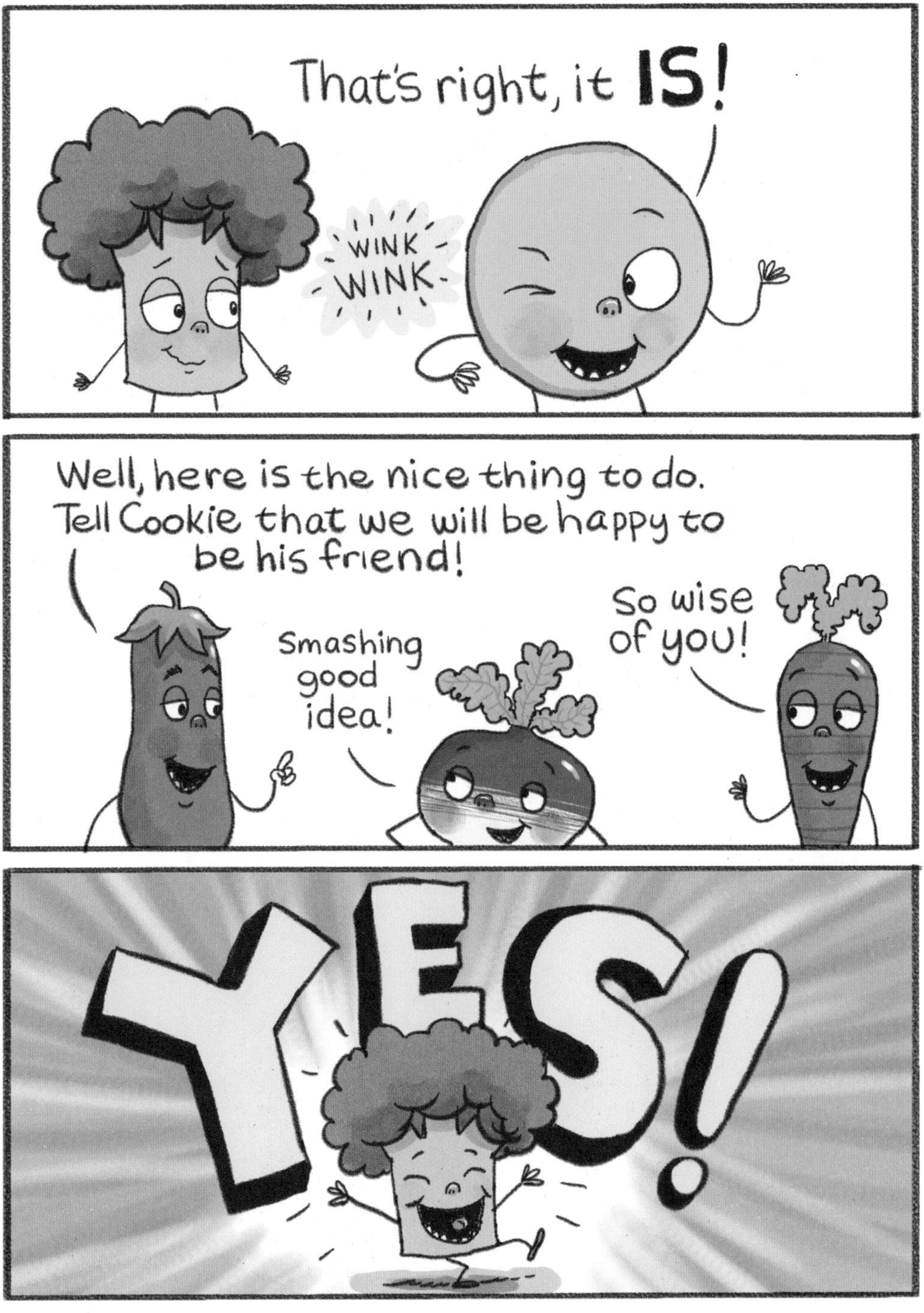
That's right, it IS!
WINK WINK
Well, here is the nice thing to do. Tell Cookie that we will be happy to be his friend!
Smashing good idea!
So wise of you!
YES!

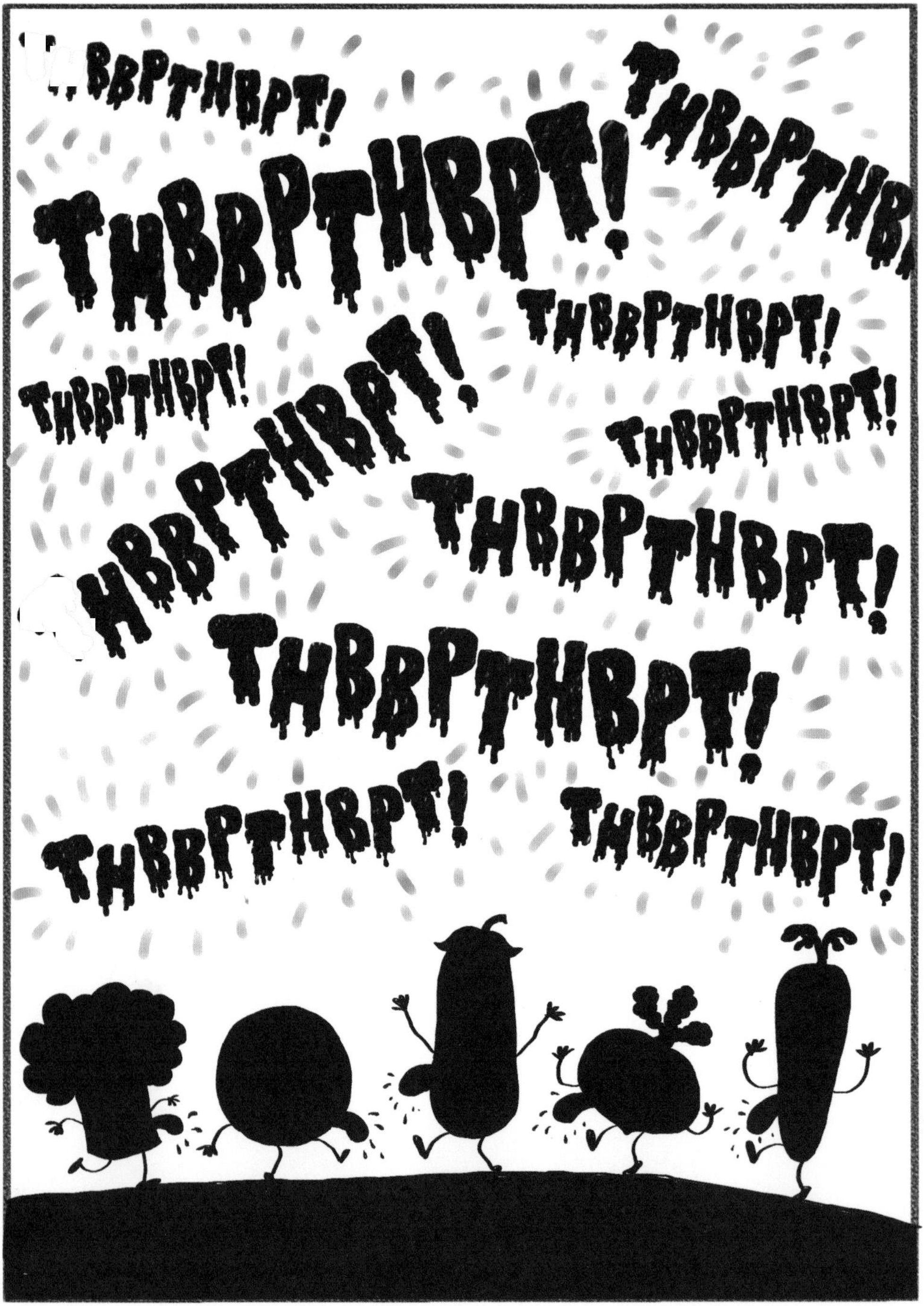
THBBPTHBPT!
THBBPTHBPT!
THBBPTHBPT!
THBBPTHBPT!
THBBPTHBPT!
THBBPTHBPT!
THBBPTHBPT!
THBBPTHBPT!
THBBPTHBPT!

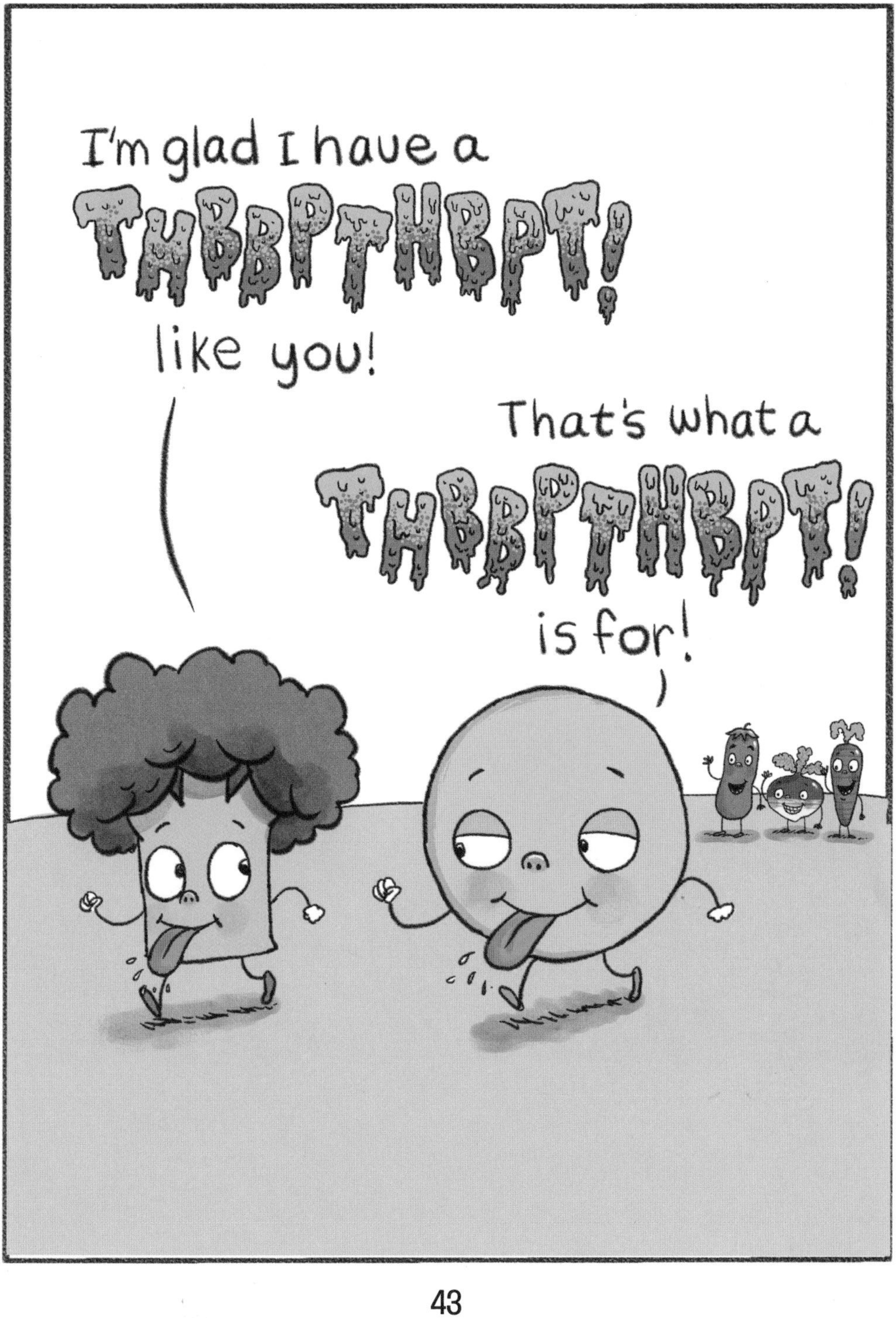
I'm glad I have a THBBPTHBPT! like you!
That's what a THBBPTHBPT! is for!

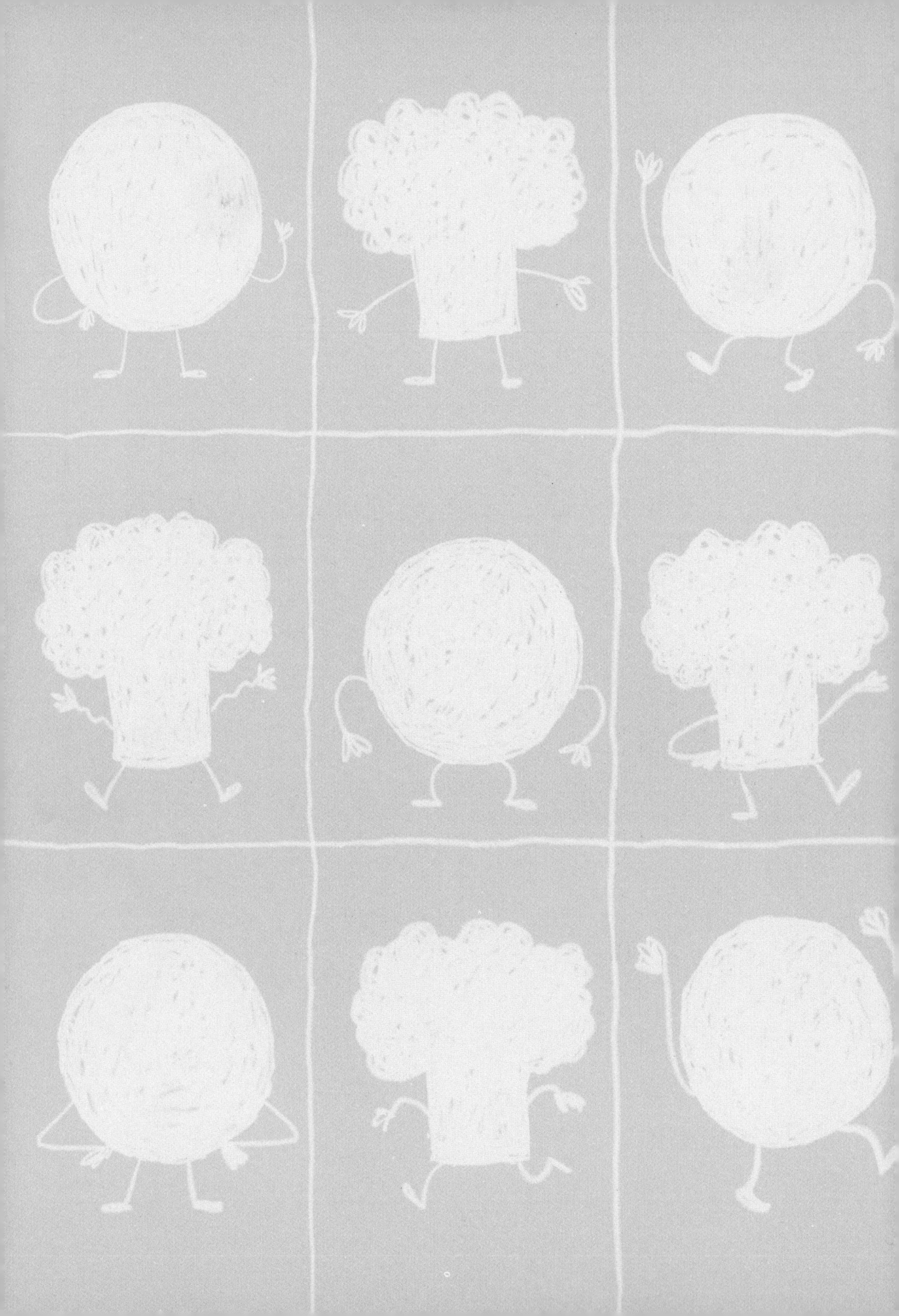

Chapter 3

WHERE DID BROCCOLI GO?

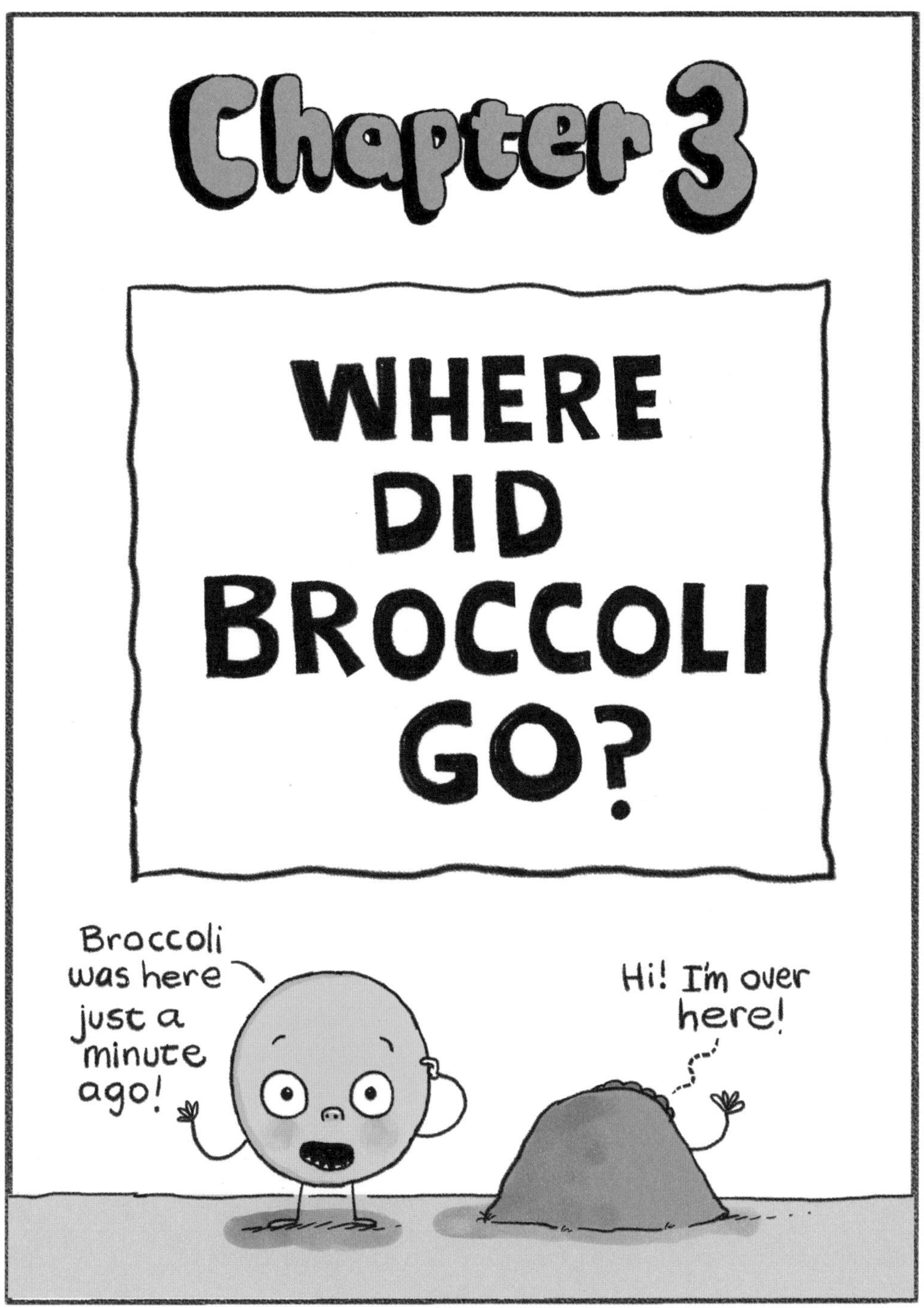
Broccoli was here just a minute ago!
Hi! I'm over here!

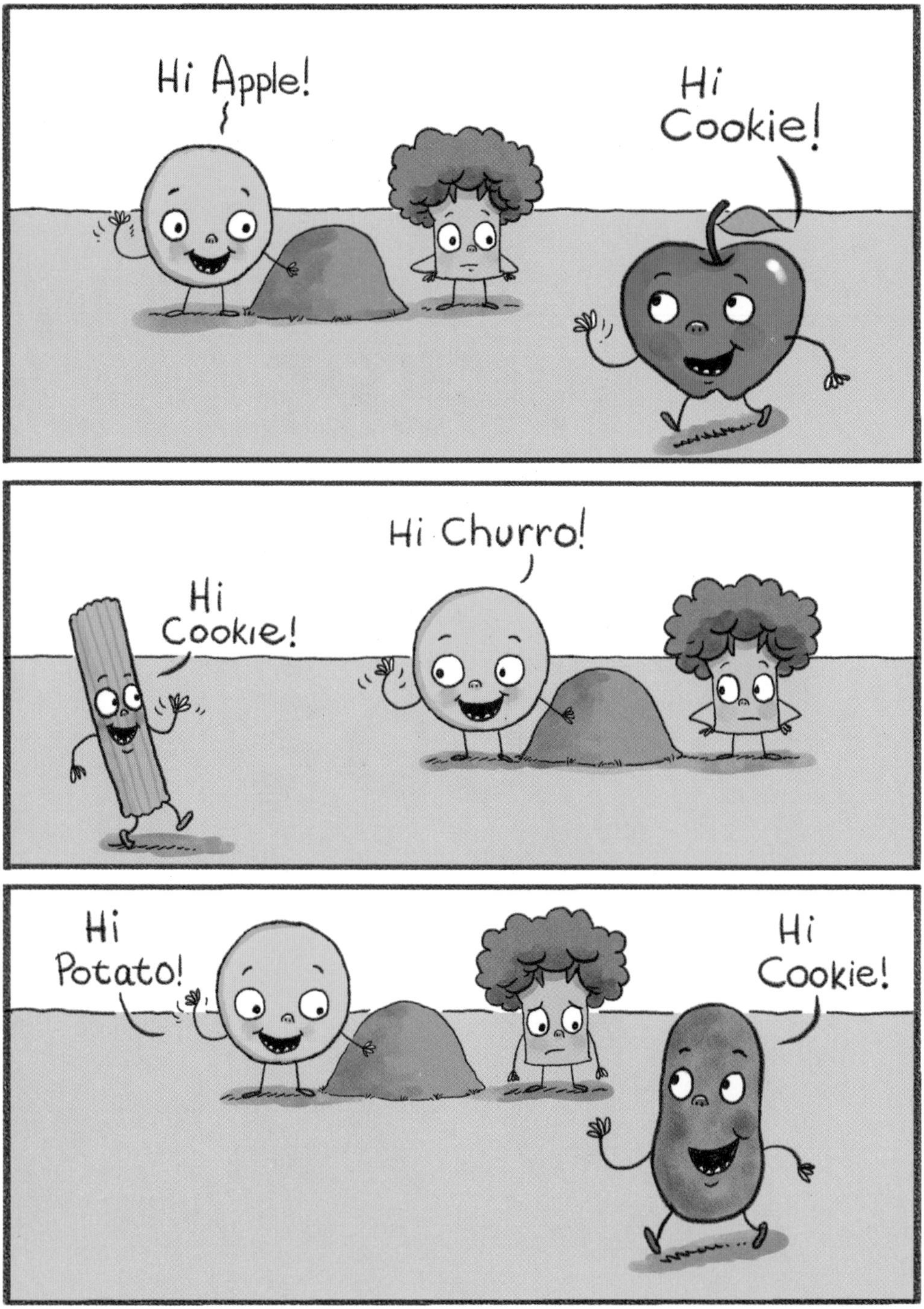
Hi Apple!
Hi Cookie!
Hi Churro!
Hi Cookie!
Hi Potato!
Hi Cookie!

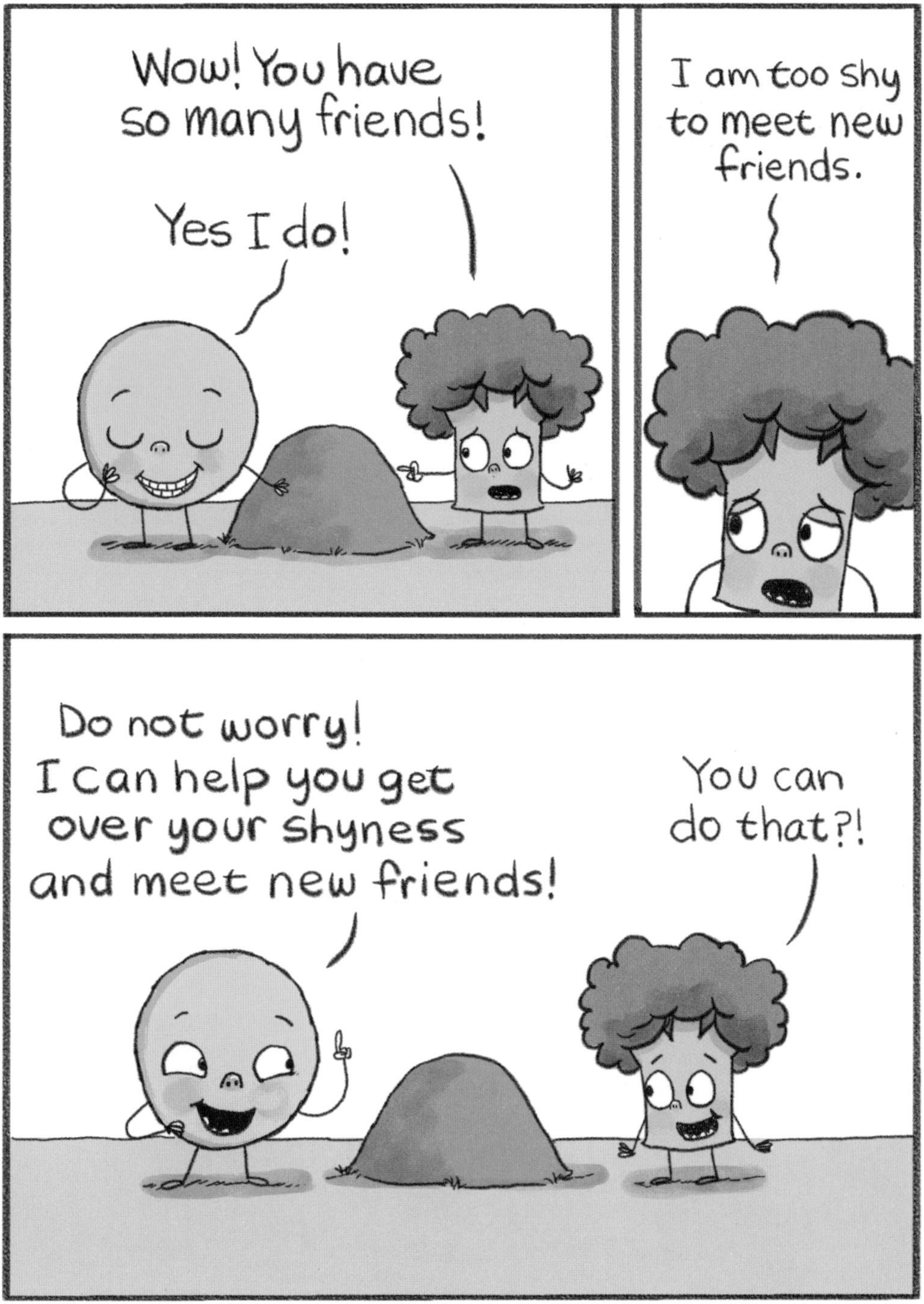
Wow! You have so many friends!
Yes I do!
I am too shy to meet new friends.
Do not worry! I can help you get over your shyness and meet new friends!
You can do that?!

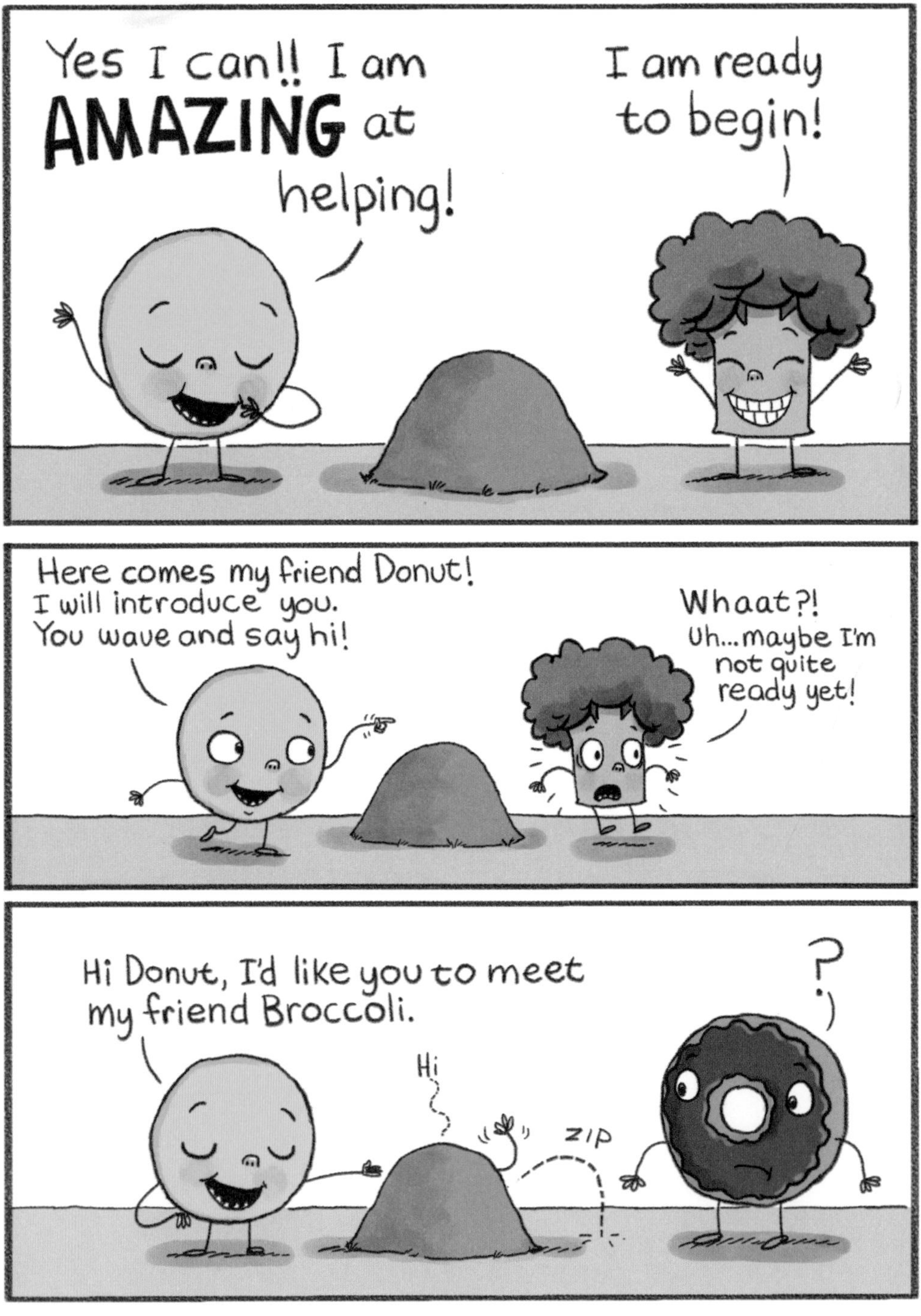

Yes I can!! I am AMAZING at helping!
I am ready to begin!
Here comes my friend Donut! I will introduce you. You wave and say hi!
Whaat?! Uh...maybe I'm not quite ready yet!
Hi Donut, I'd like you to meet my friend Broccoli.
Hi
ZIP
?

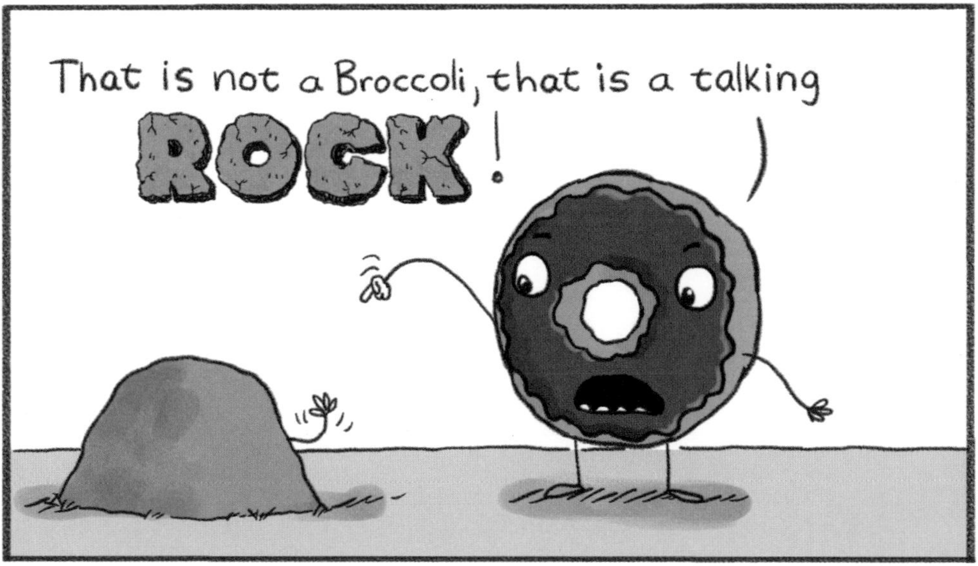
That is not a Broccoli, that is a talking
ROCK!

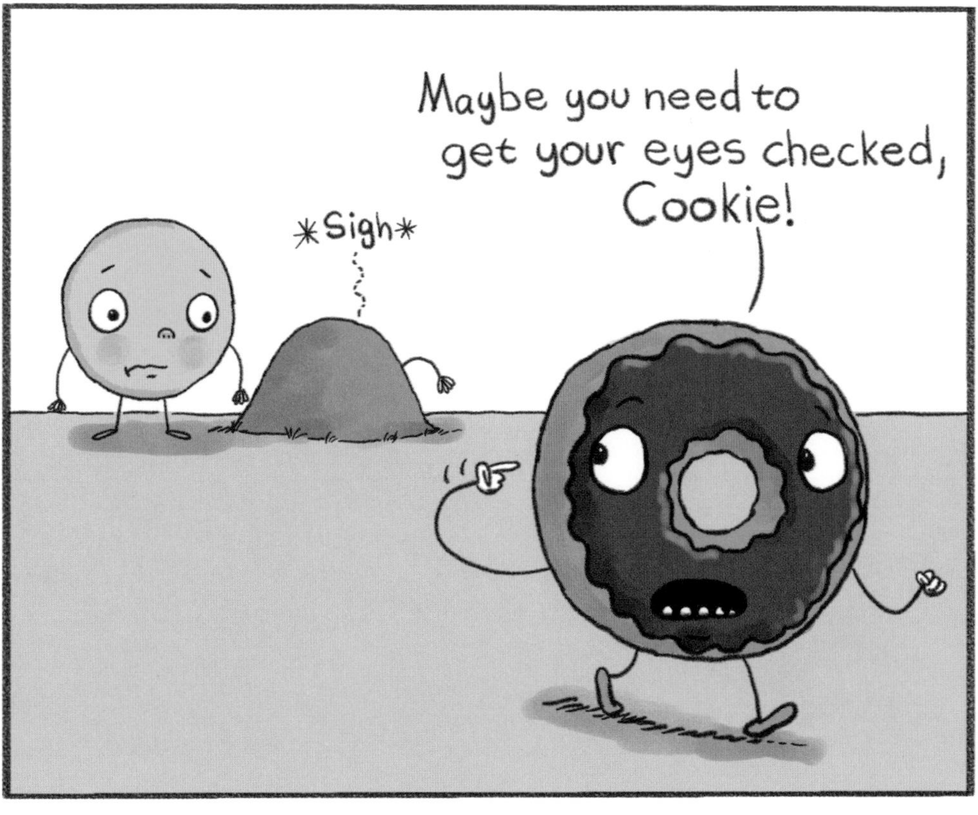
Maybe you need to get your eyes checked, Cookie!
Sigh

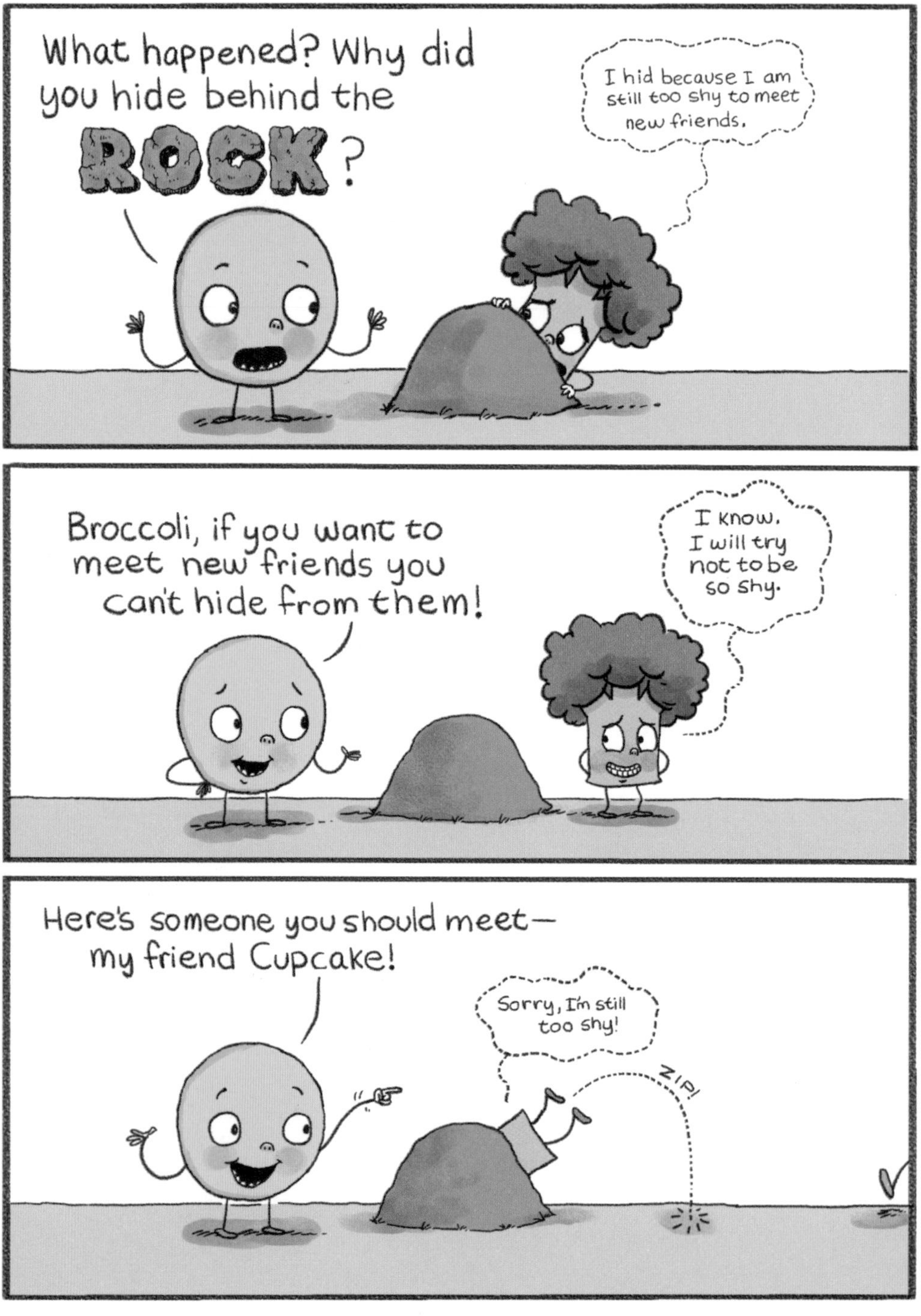
What happened? Why did you hide behind the ROCK?
I hid because I am still too shy to meet new friends.
Broccoli, if you want to meet new friends you can't hide from them!
I know. I will try not to be so shy.
Here's someone you should meet— my friend Cupcake!
Sorry, I'm still too shy!
ZIP!

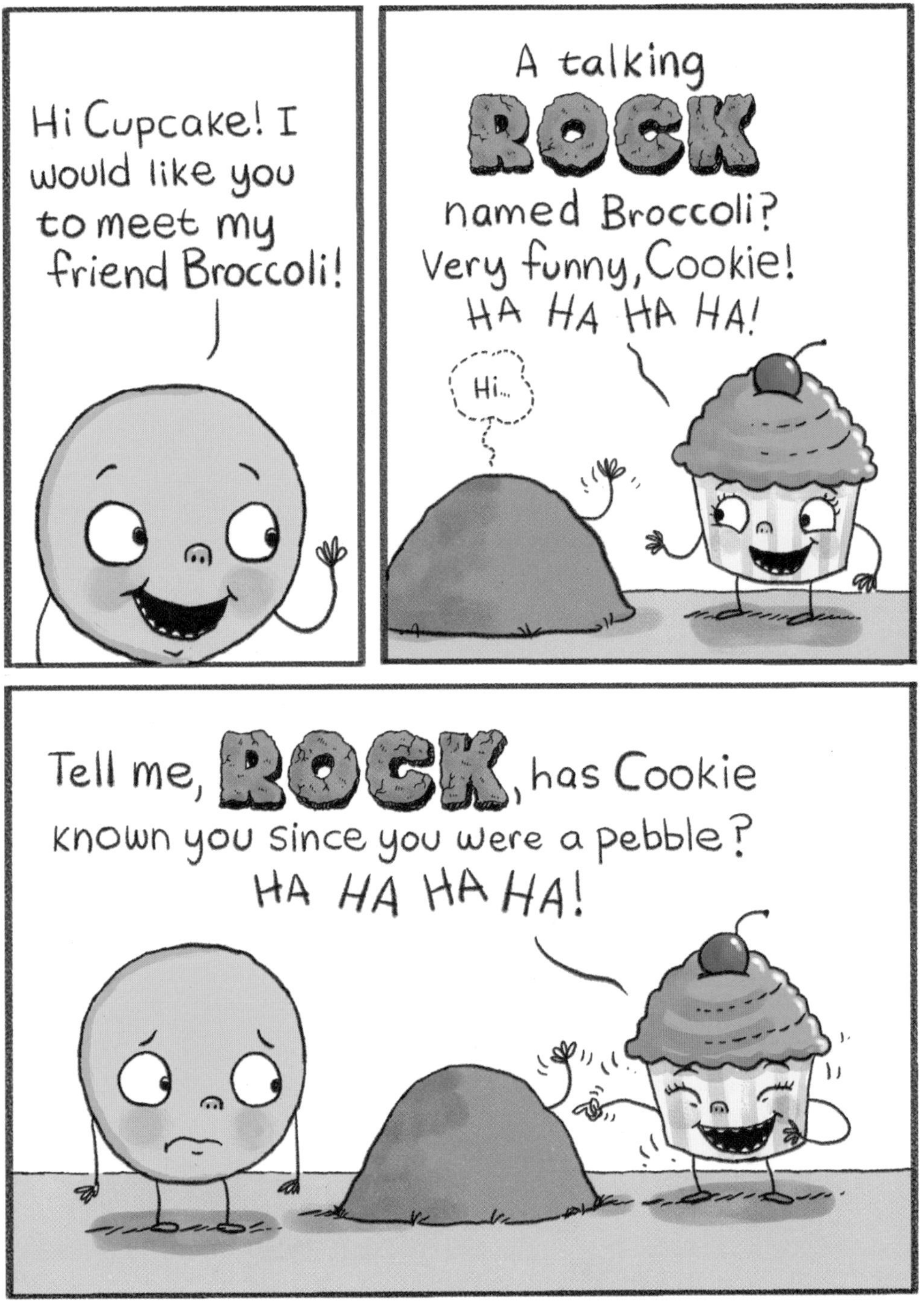
Hi Cupcake! I would like you to meet my friend Broccoli!
A talking ROCK named Broccoli? Very funny, Cookie! HA HA HA HA!
Hi...
Tell me, ROCK, has Cookie known you since you were a pebble? HA HA HA HA!

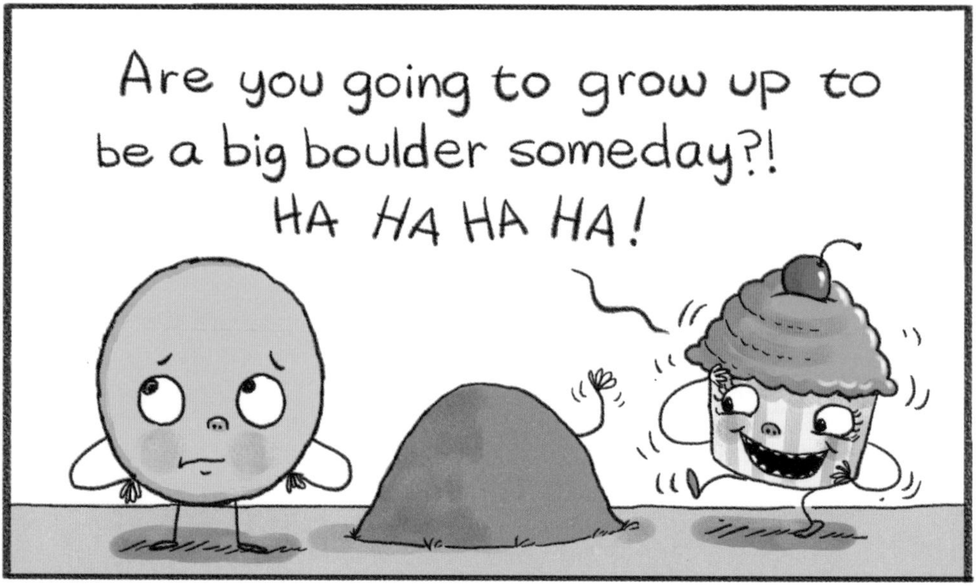
Are you going to grow up to be a big boulder someday?! HA HA HA HA!

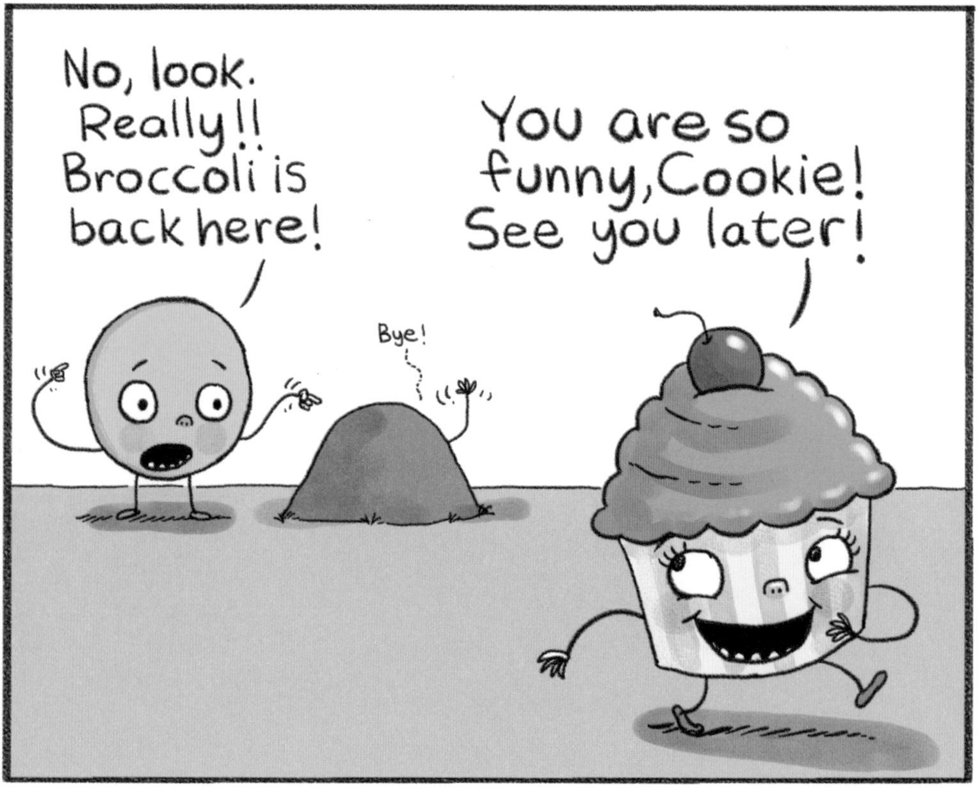
No, look. Really!! Broccoli is back here!
Bye!
You are so funny, Cookie! See you later!

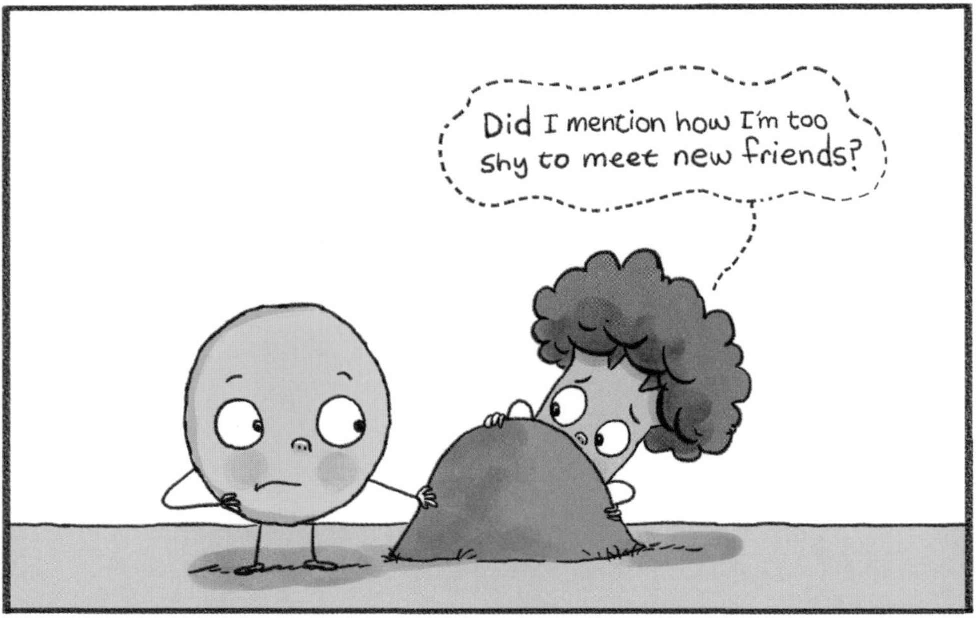
Did I mention how I'm too shy to meet new friends?

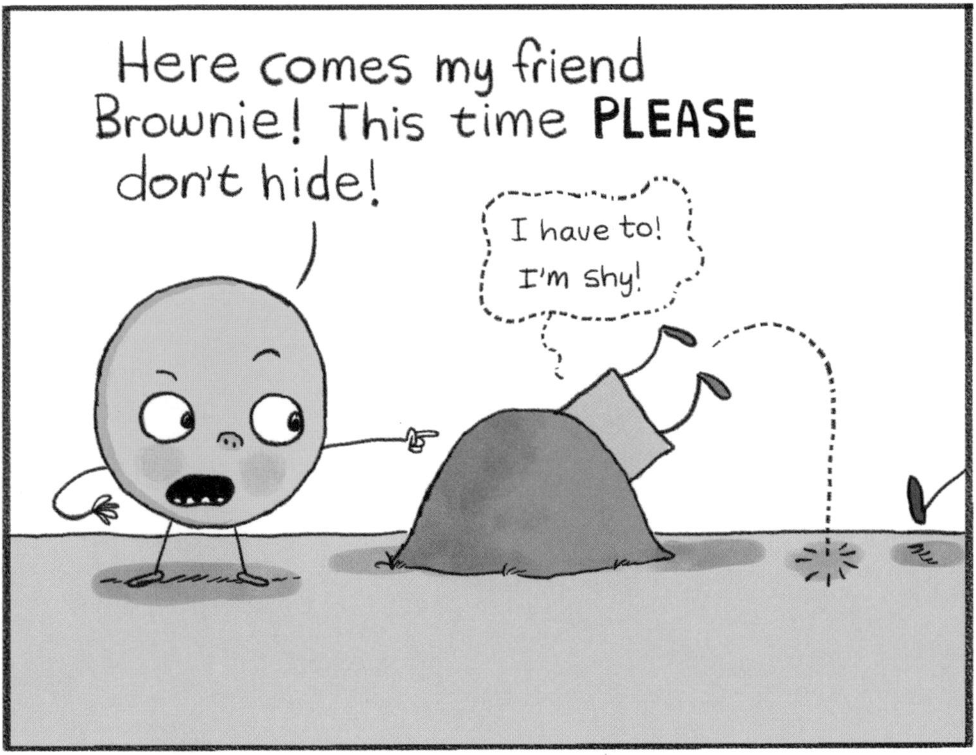
Here comes my friend Brownie! This time **PLEASE** don't hide!
I have to! I'm shy!

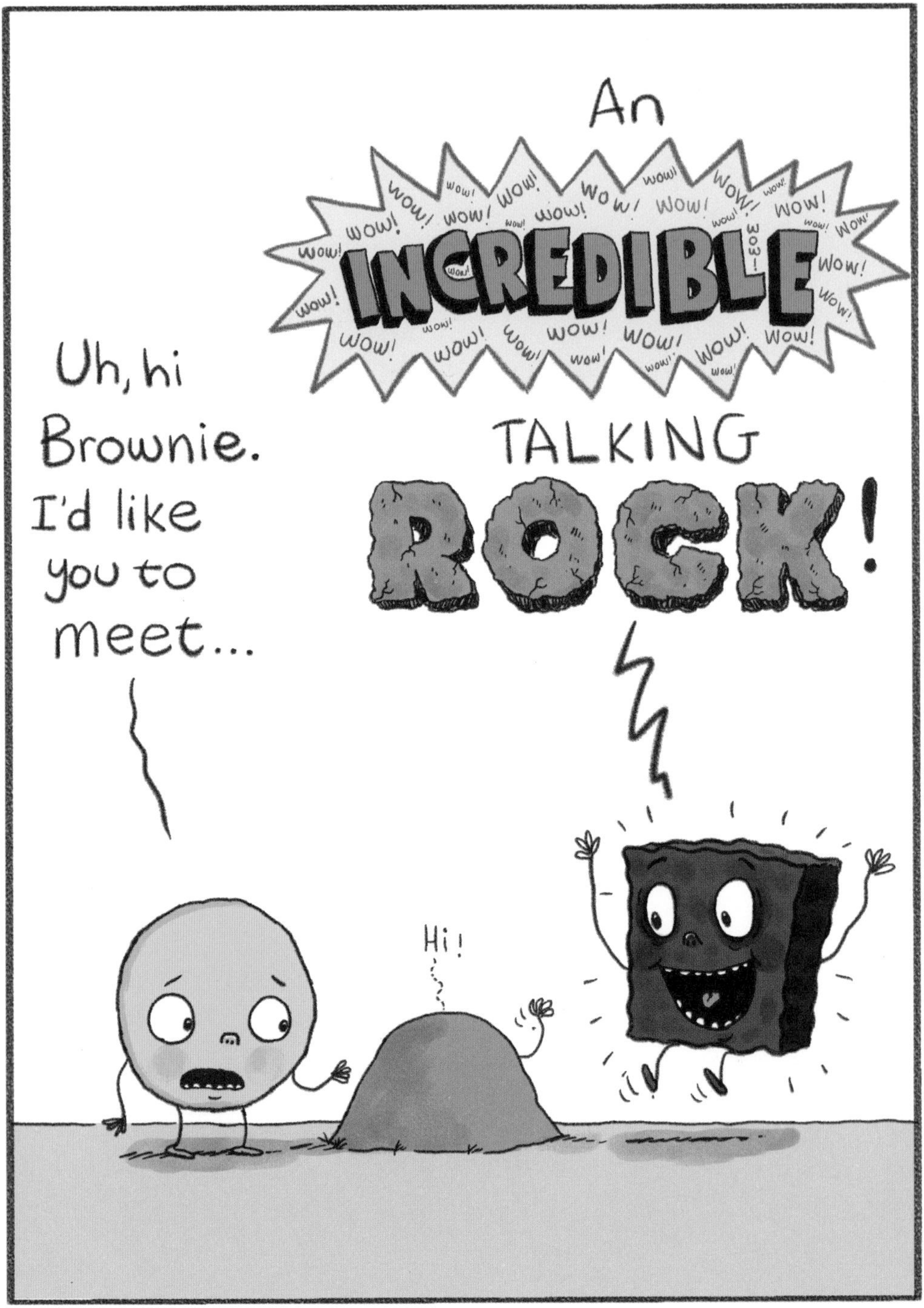
Uh, hi Brownie. I'd like you to meet...
An INCREDIBLE TALKING ROCK!
Hi!

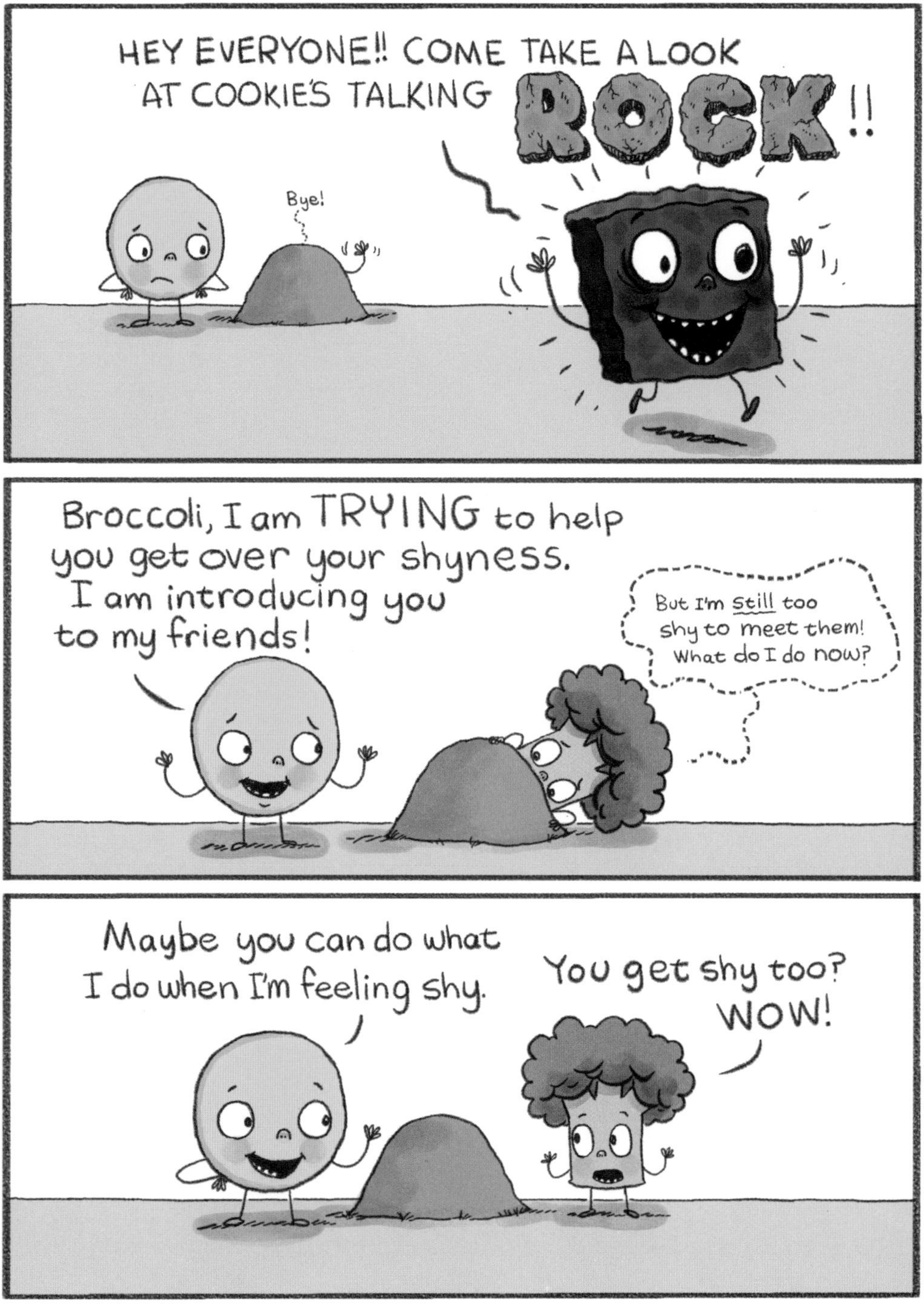

HEY EVERYONE!! COME TAKE A LOOK AT COOKIE'S TALKING ROCK!!
Bye!
Broccoli, I am TRYING to help you get over your shyness. I am introducing you to my friends!
But I'm still too shy to meet them! What do I do now?
Maybe you can do what I do when I'm feeling shy.
You get shy too? WOW!

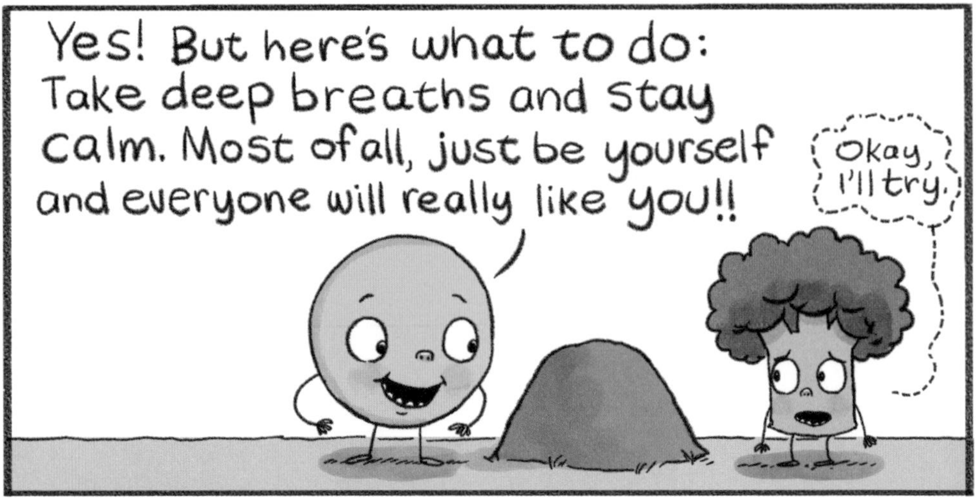
Yes! But here's what to do: Take deep breaths and stay calm. Most of all, just be yourself and everyone will really like you!!
Okay, I'll try.

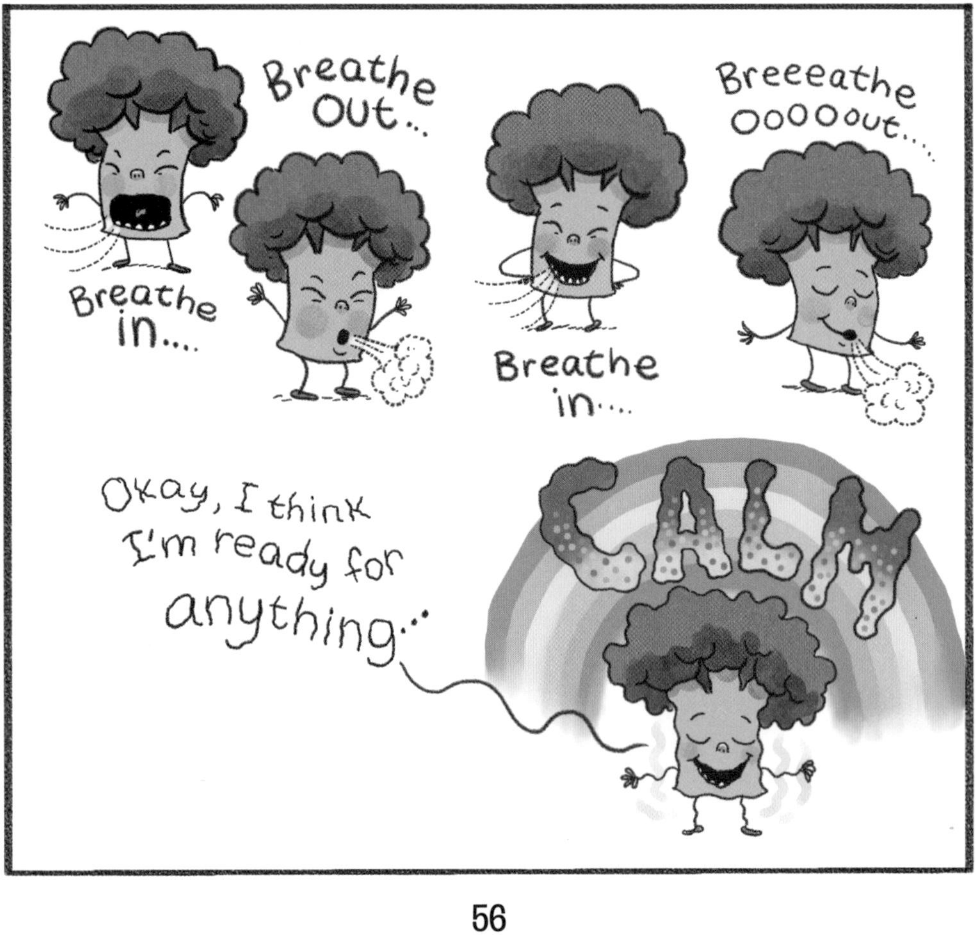
Breathe in....
Breathe out...
Breathe in....
Breeeathe ooooout.....
CALM
Okay, I think I'm ready for anything...

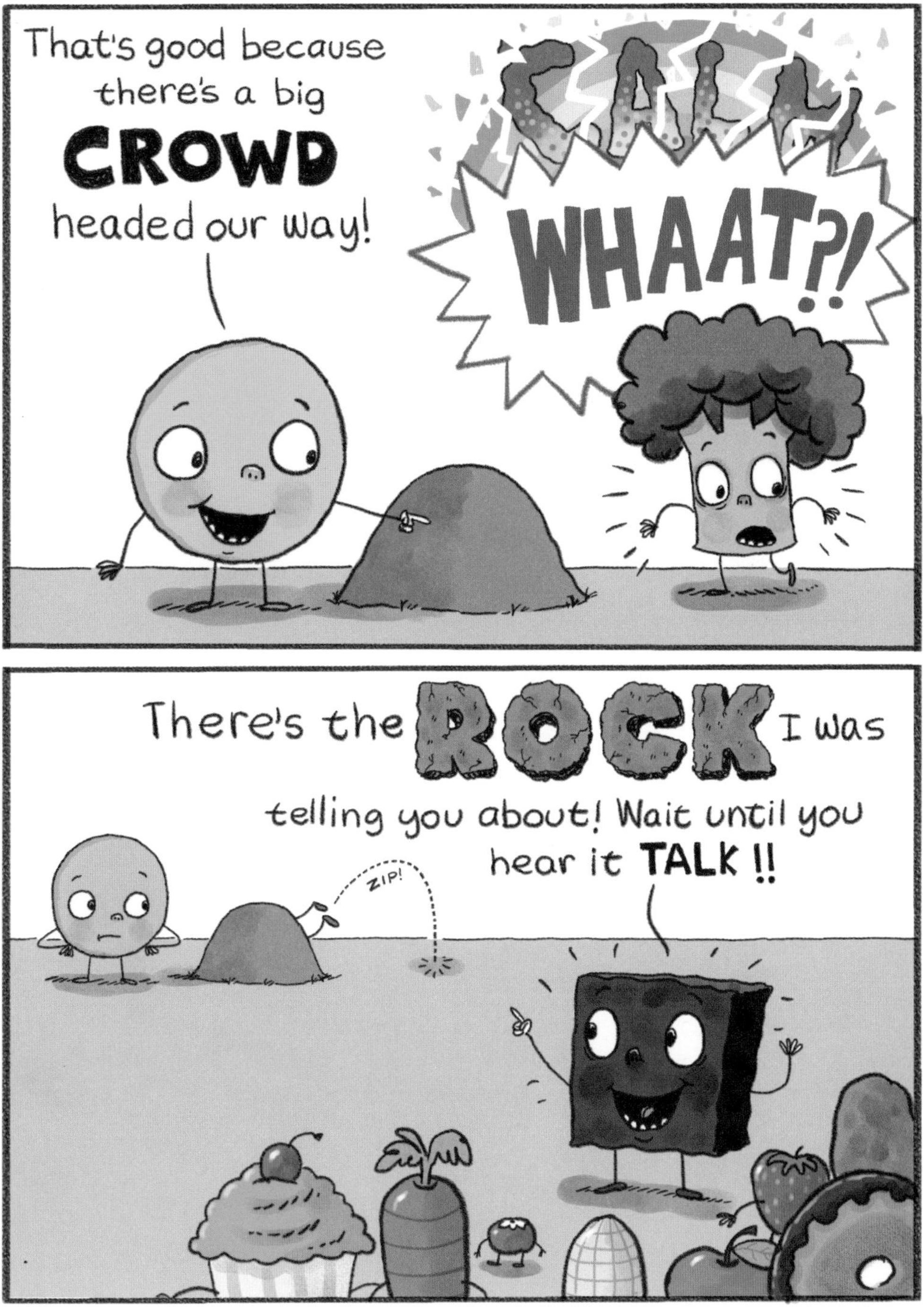
That's good because there's a big CROWD headed our way!
WHAAT?!
There's the ROCK I was telling you about! Wait until you hear it TALK!!
ZIP!

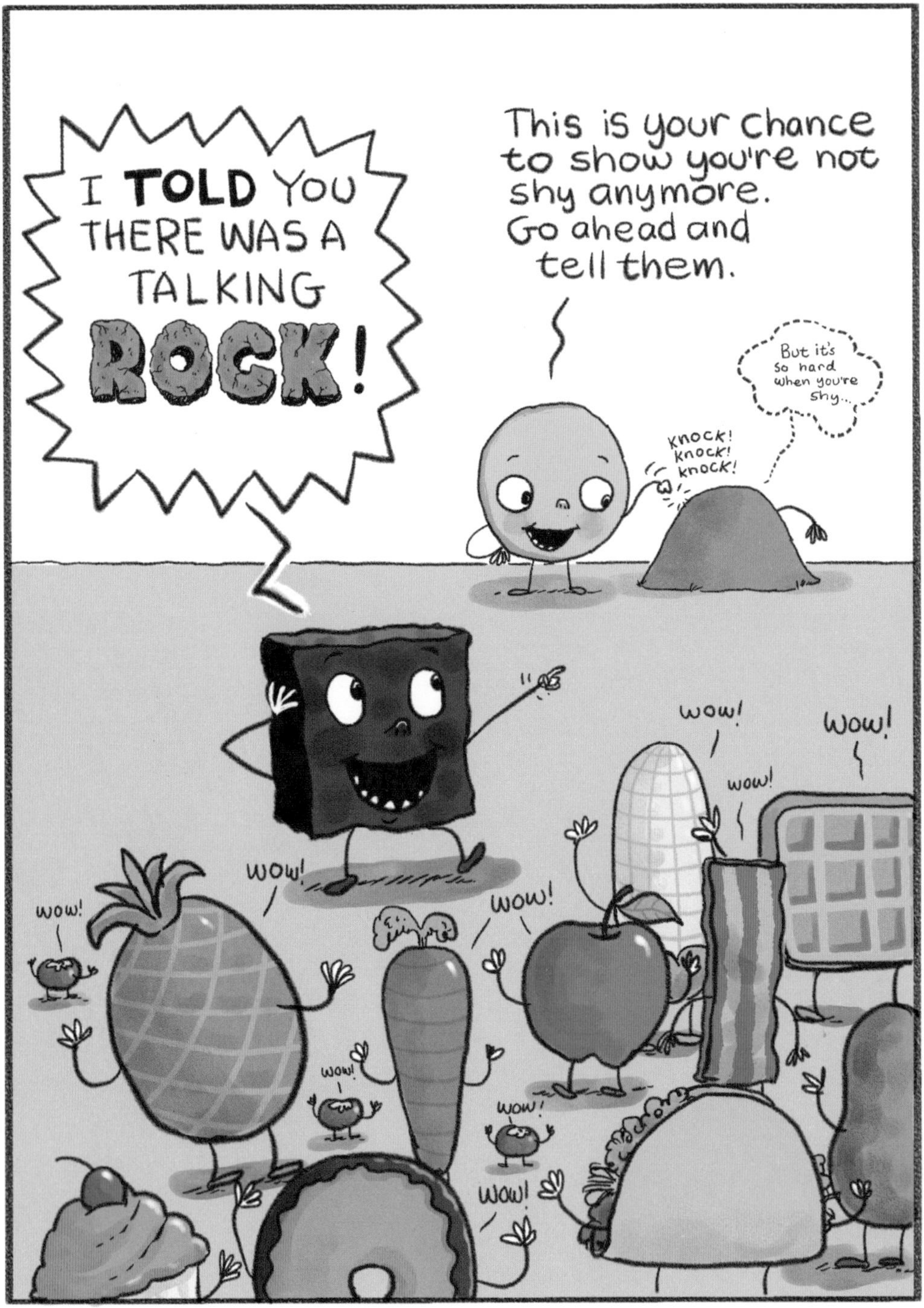

I TOLD YOU THERE WAS A TALKING ROCK!
This is your chance to show you're not shy anymore. Go ahead and tell them.
Knock! Knock! Knock!
But it's so hard when you're shy...
WOW!
WOW!
WOW!
WOW!
WOW!
WOW!
WOW!
WOW!
WOW!

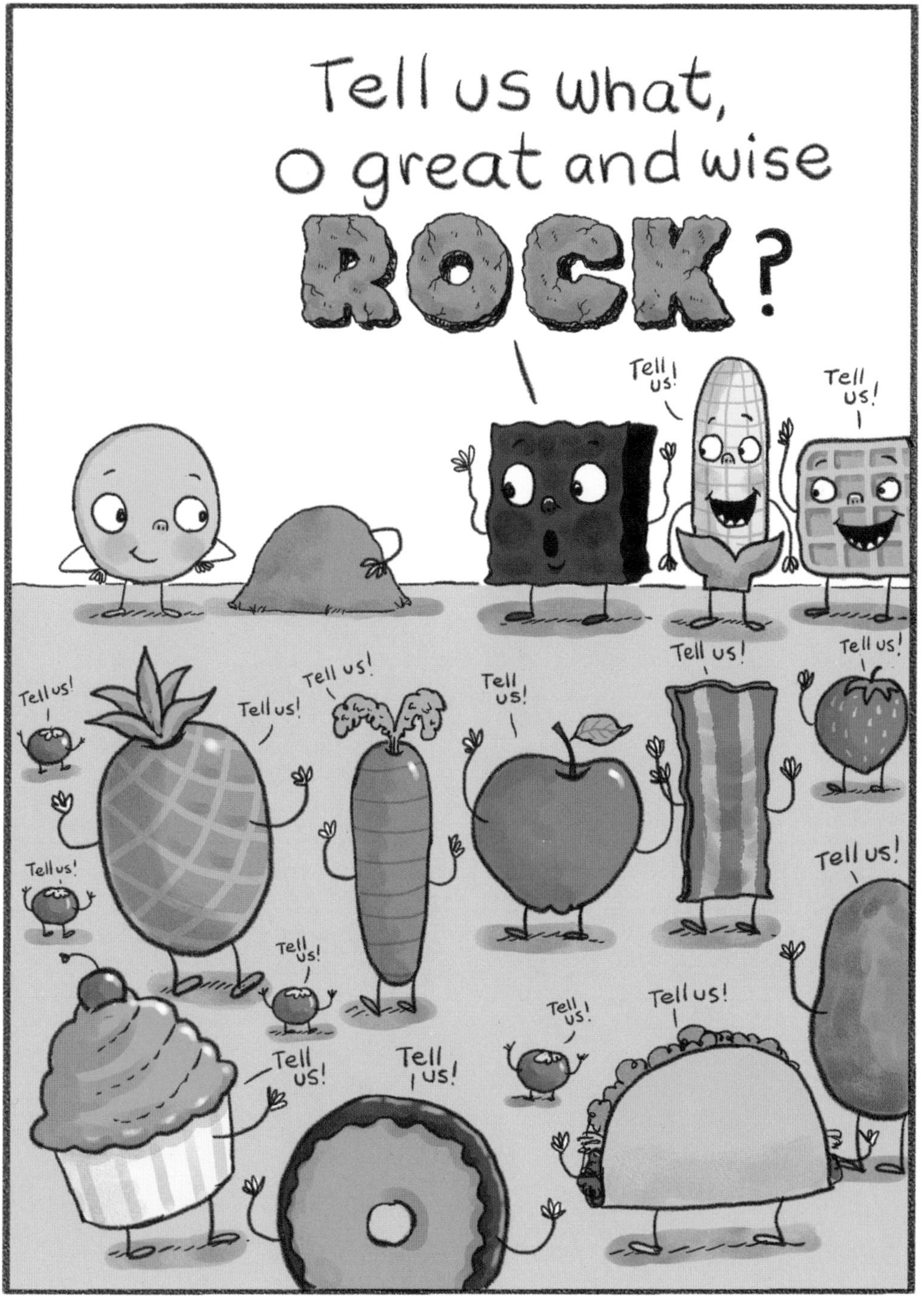
Tell us what,
O great and wise
ROCK?
Tell us!
Tell us!
Tell us!
Tell us!
Tell us!
Tell us!
Tell us!
Tell us!
Tell us!
Tell us!
Tell us!
Tell us!
Tell us!
Tell us!
Tell us!
Tell us!

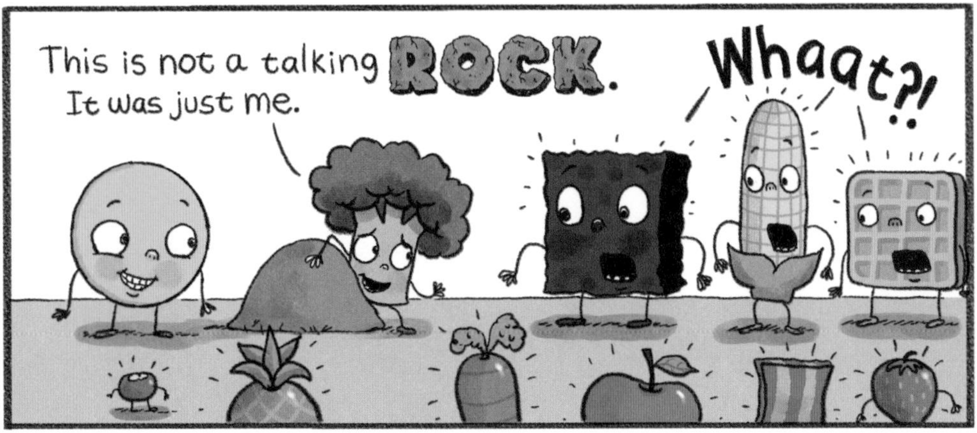
This is not a talking ROCK.
It was just me.
Whaaat?!
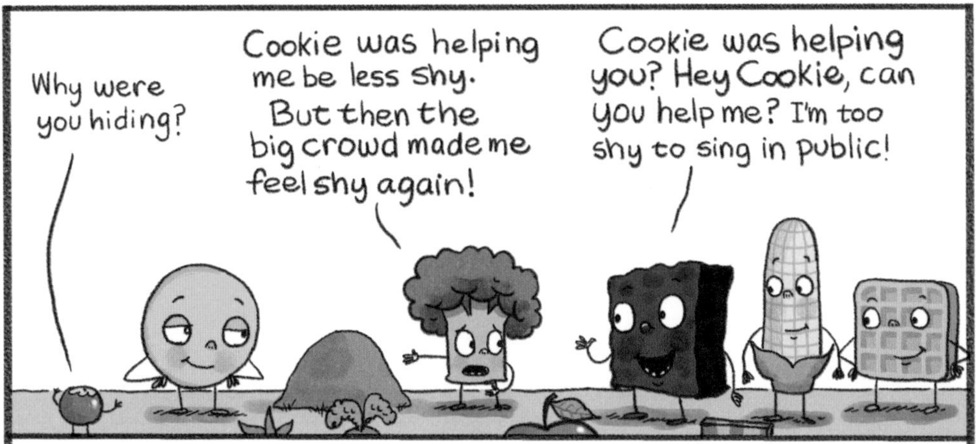
Why were you hiding?
Cookie was helping me be less shy. But then the big crowd made me feel shy again!
Cookie was helping you? Hey Cookie, can you help me? I'm too shy to sing in public!
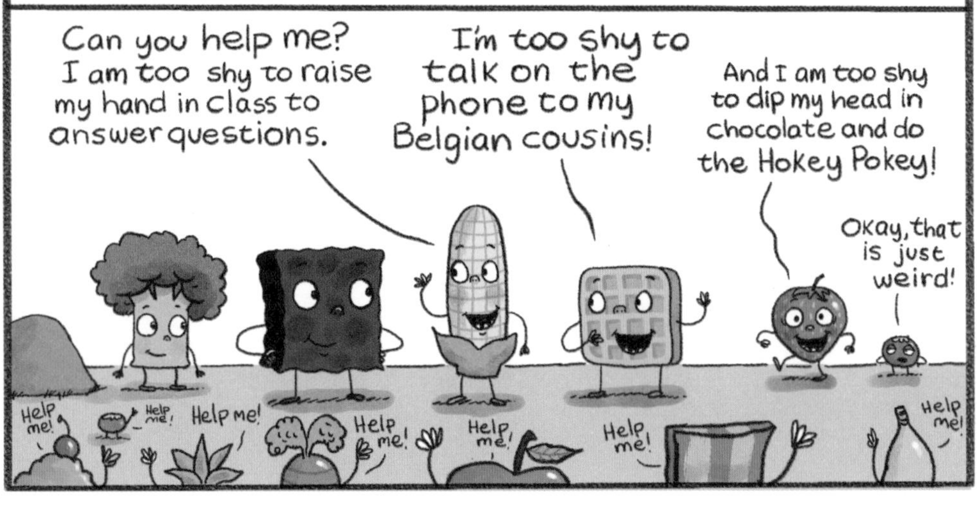
Can you help me? I am too shy to raise my hand in class to answer questions.
I'm too shy to talk on the phone to my Belgian cousins!
And I am too shy to dip my head in chocolate and do the Hokey Pokey!
Okay, that is just weird!
Help me!
Help me!
Help me!
Help me!
Help me!
Help me!
Help me!

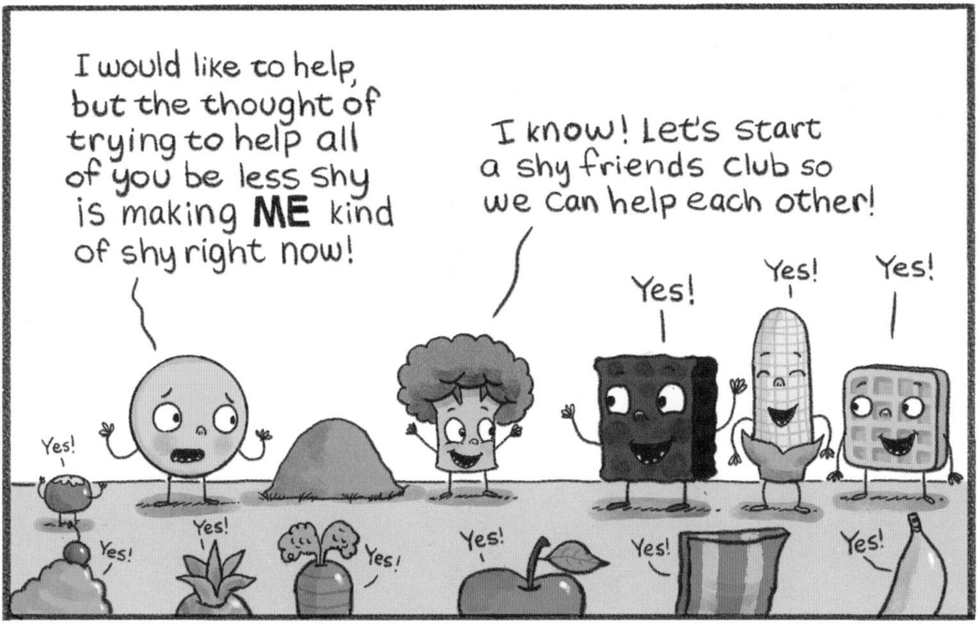
I would like to help, but the thought of trying to help all of you be less shy is making **ME** kind of shy right now!
I know! Let's start a shy friends club so we can help each other!
Yes!
Yes!
Yes!
Yes!
Yes!
Yes!
Yes!
Yes!
Yes!
Yes!

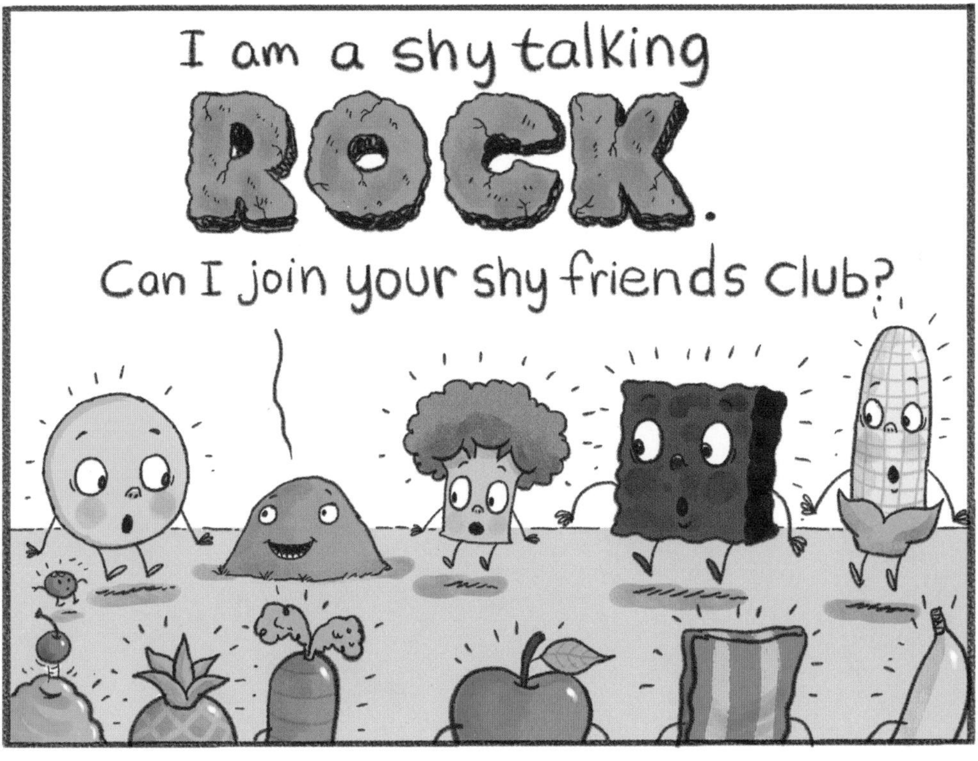
I am a shy talking
ROCK.
Can I join your shy friends club?

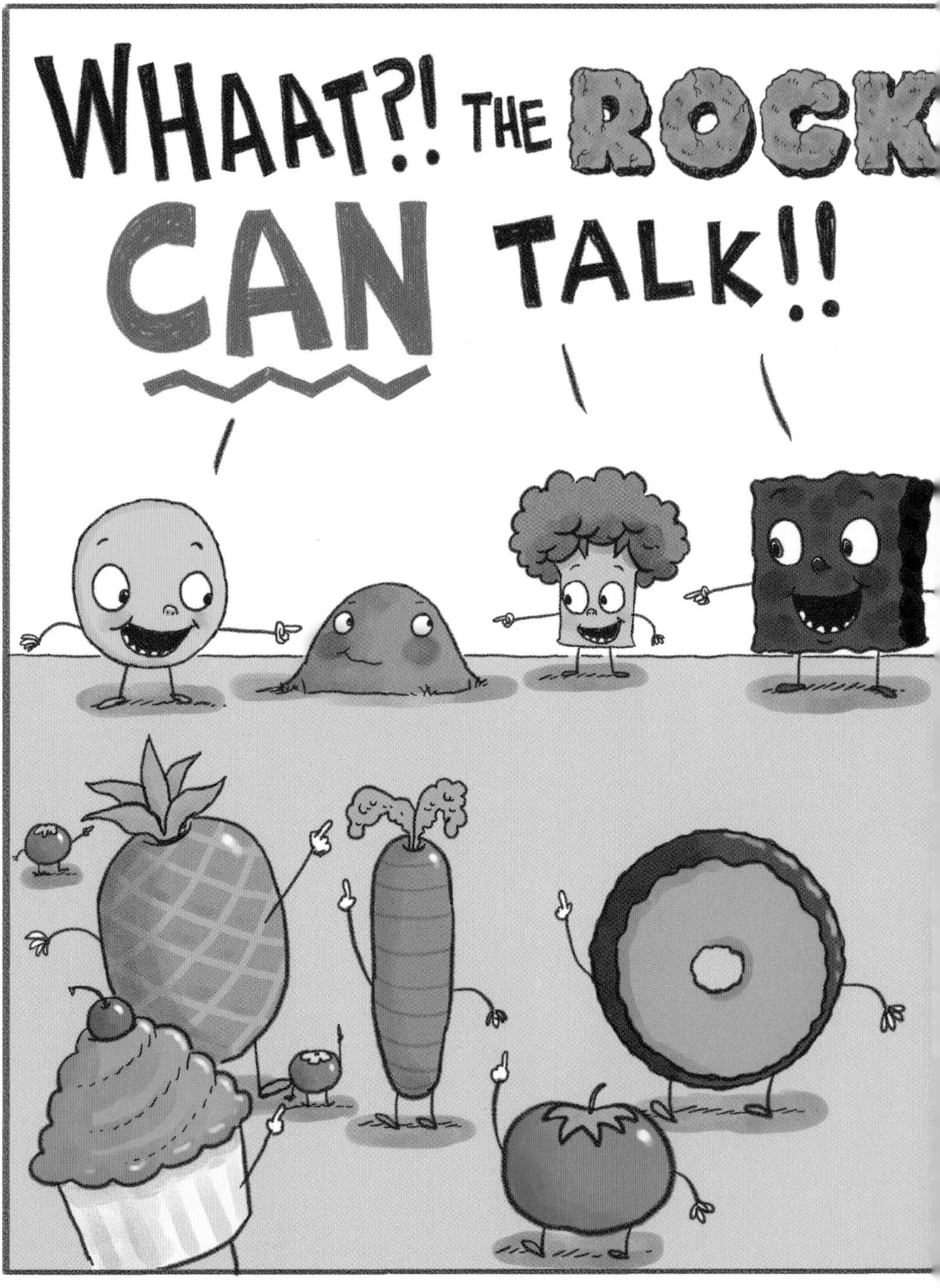
WHAAT?! THE ROCK
CAN TALK!!

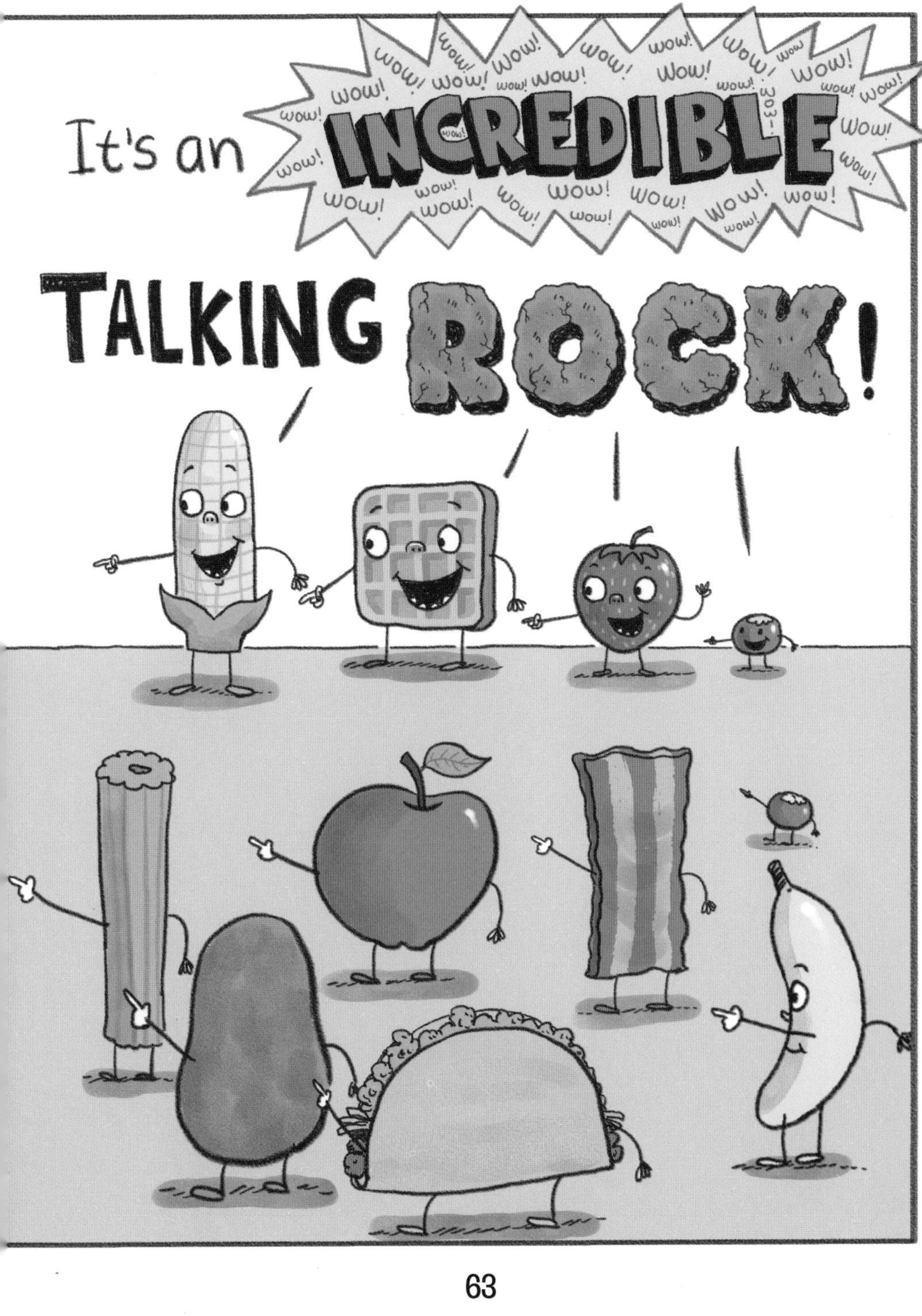
It's an INCREDIBLE TALKING ROCK!

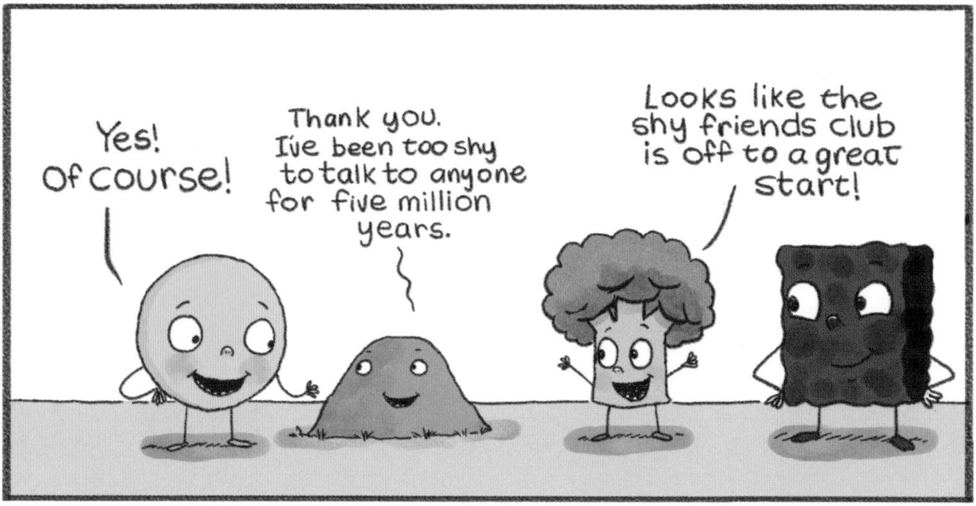
Yes! Of course!
Thank you. I've been too shy to talk to anyone for five million years.
Looks like the shy friends club is off to a great start!

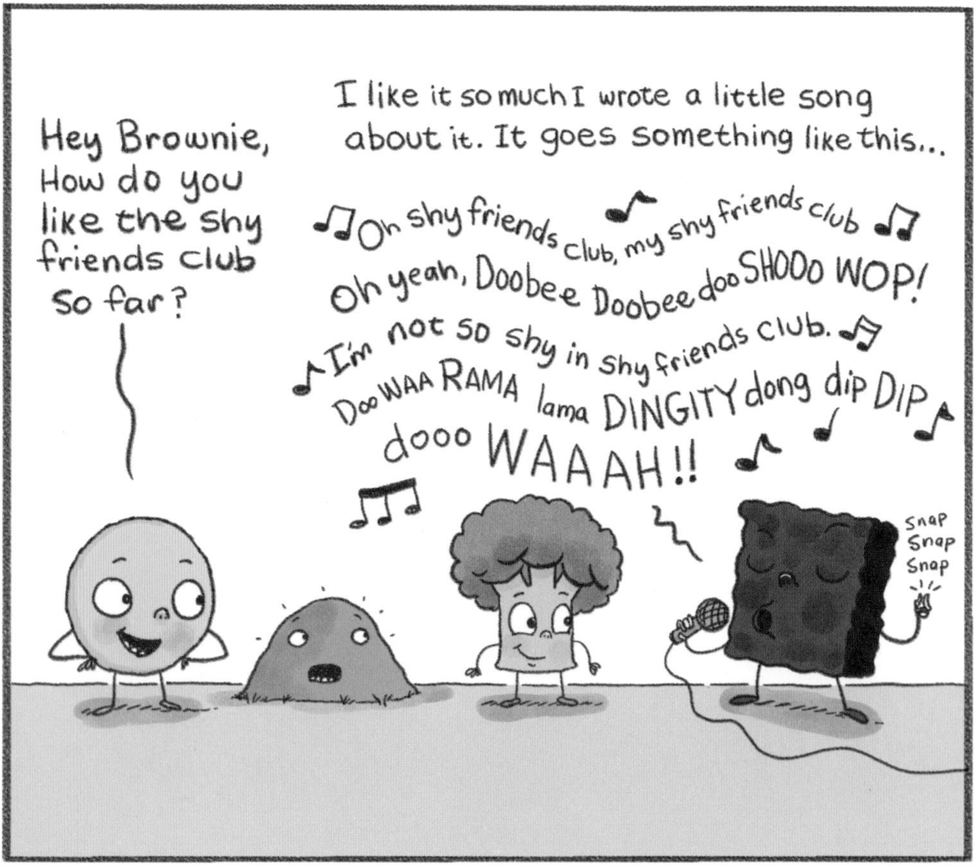
Hey Brownie, How do you like the shy friends club so far?
I like it so much I wrote a little song about it. It goes something like this...
Oh shy friends club, my shy friends club
Oh yeah, Doobee Doobee doo SHOOO WOP!
I'm not so shy in shy friends club.
DooWAA RAMA lama DINGITY dong dip DIP
dooo WAAAH!!
Snap
Snap
Snap

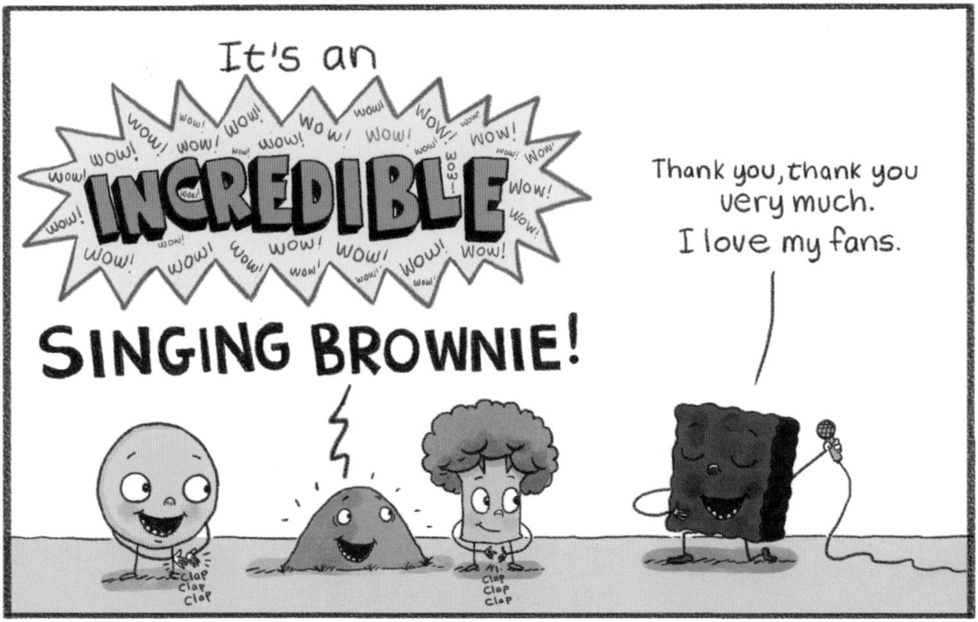
It's an
INCREDIBLE
SINGING BROWNIE!
Thank you, thank you very much. I love my fans.
Clap Clap Clap
Clap Clap Clap

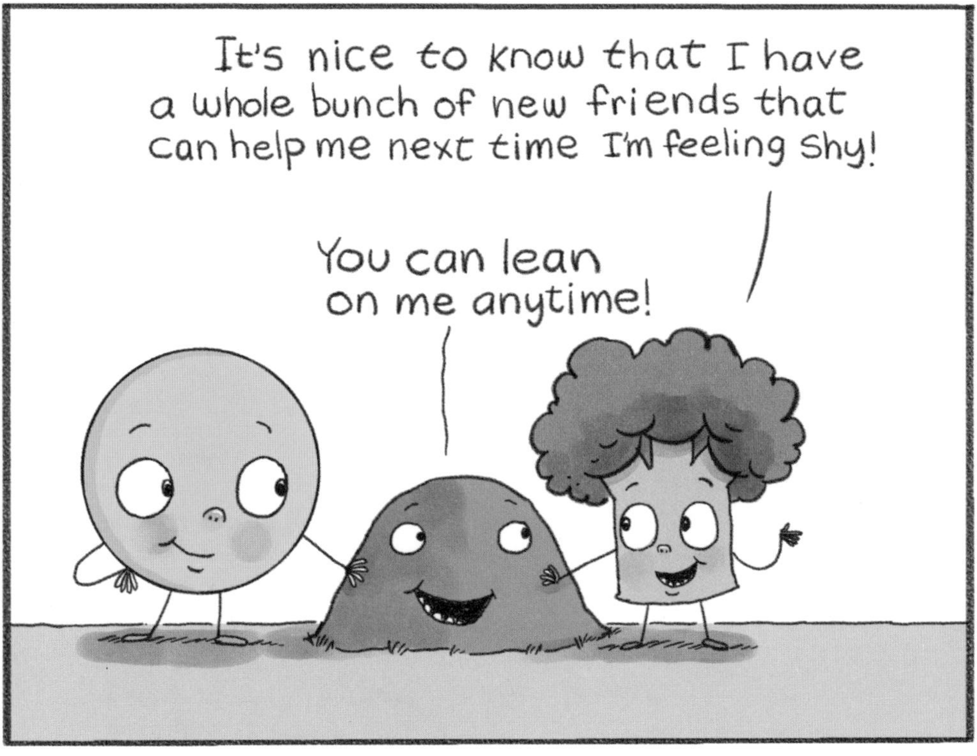
It's nice to know that I have a whole bunch of new friends that can help me next time I'm feeling shy!
You can lean on me anytime!

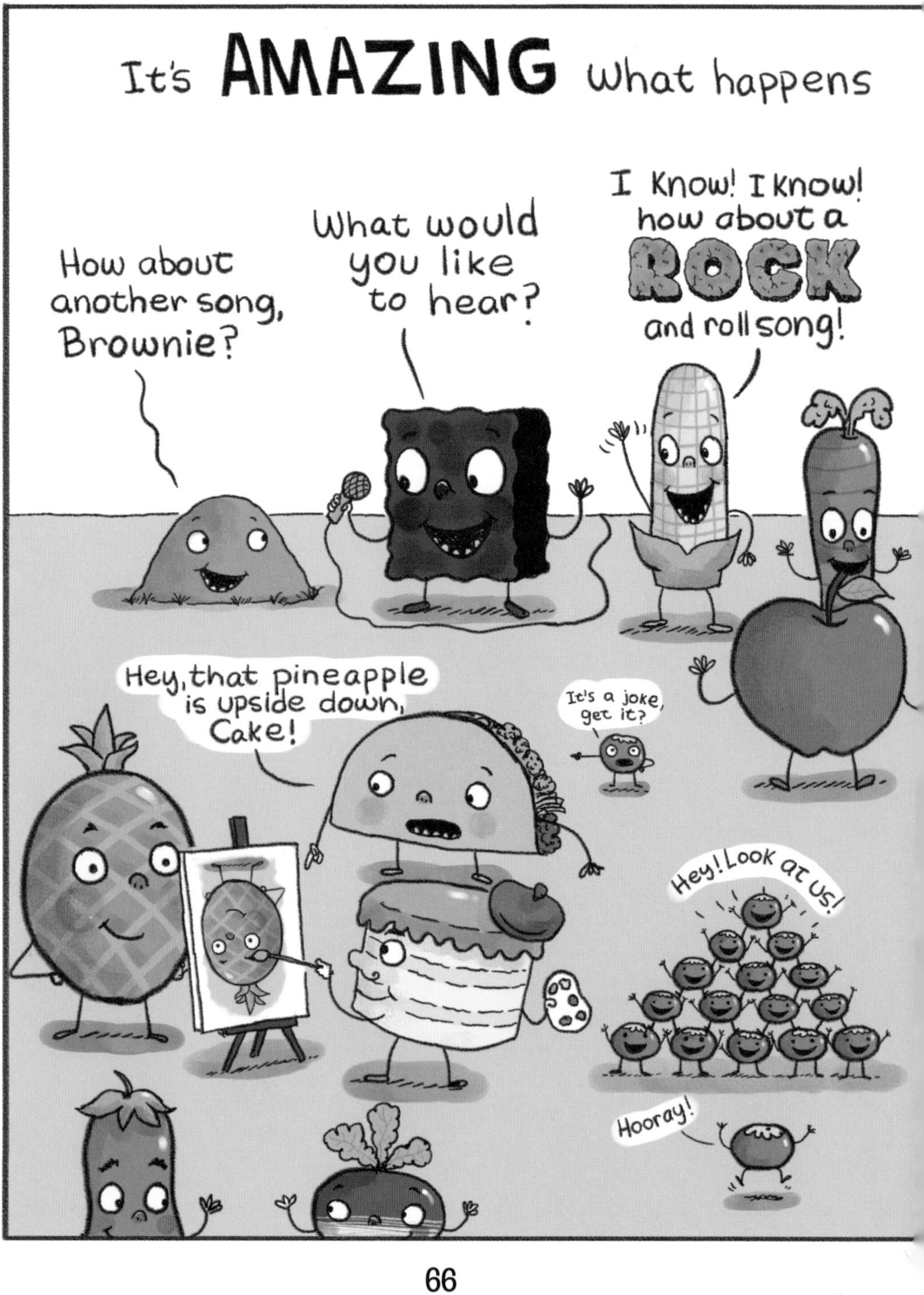
It's AMAZING what happens
How about another song, Brownie?
What would you like to hear?
I Know! I know! how about a ROCK and roll song!
Hey, that pineapple is upside down, Cake!
It's a joke, get it?
Hey! Look at us!
Hooray!

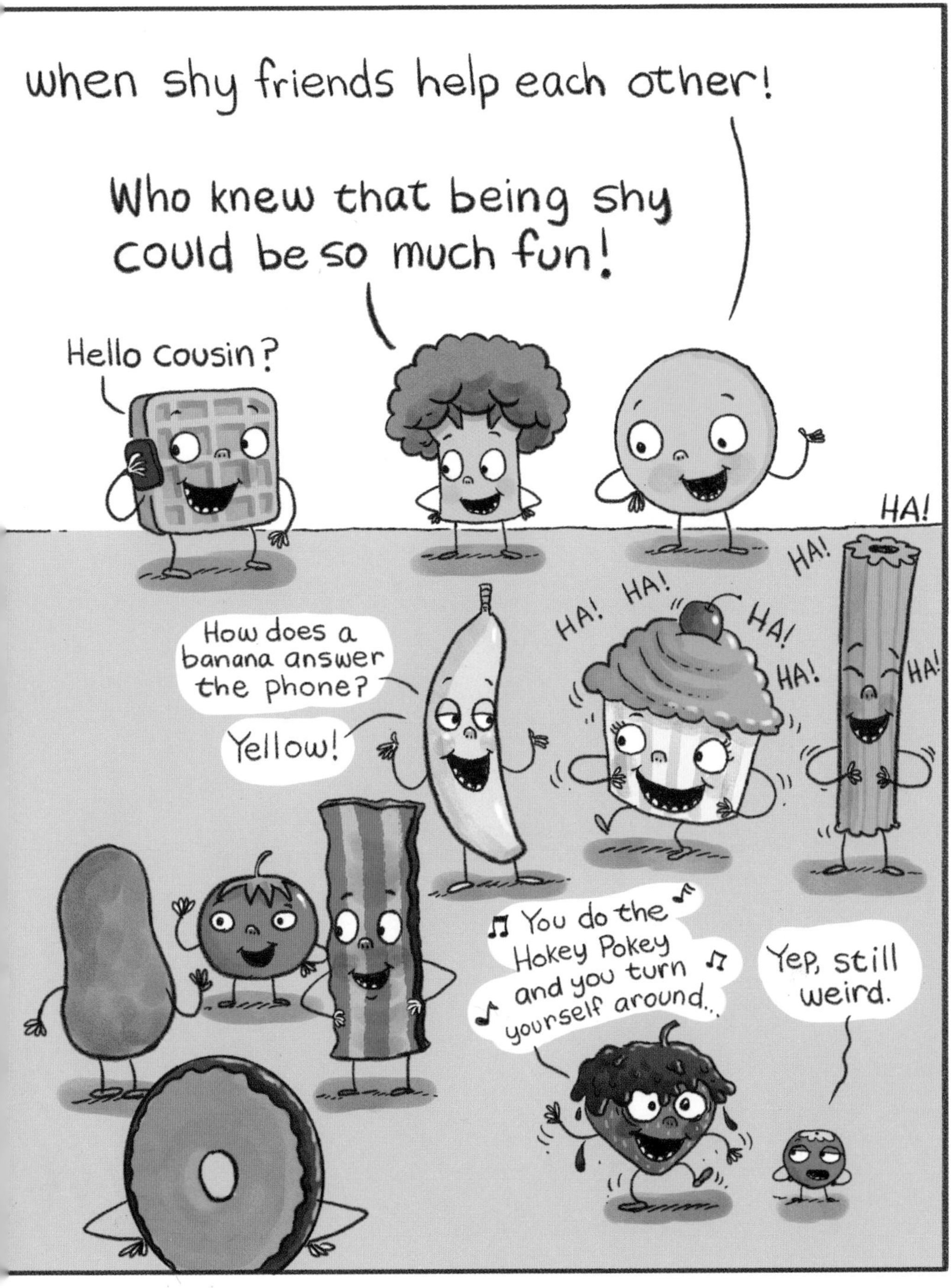
when shy friends help each other!
Who knew that being shy could be so much fun!
Hello cousin?
HA!
HA!
HA! HA!
HA!
HA!
HA!
HA!
How does a banana answer the phone?
Yellow!
You do the Hokey Pokey and you turn yourself around...
Yep, still weird.

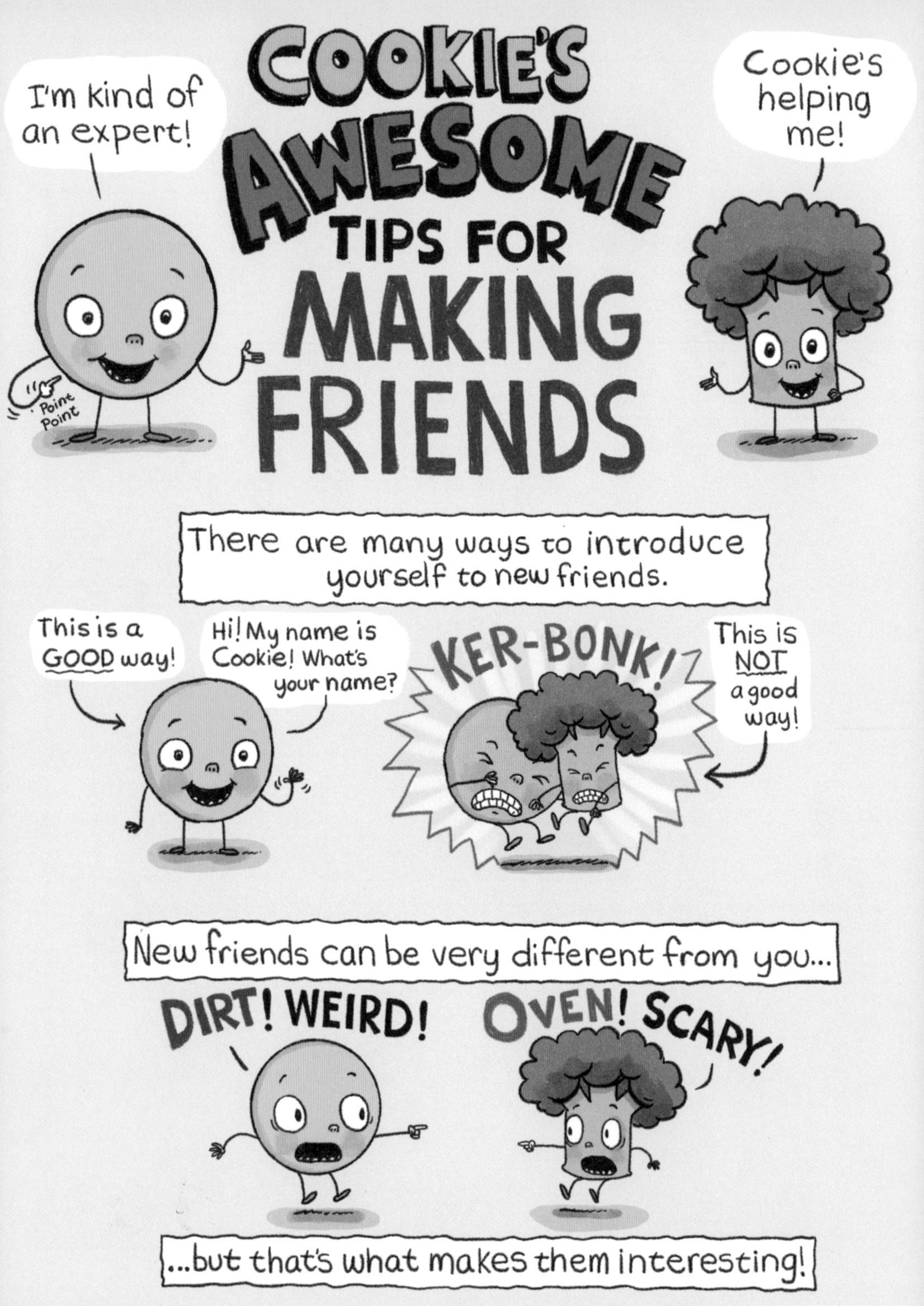

COOKIE'S AWESOME TIPS FOR MAKING FRIENDS
I'm kind of an expert!
Point Point
Cookie's helping me!
There are many ways to introduce yourself to new friends.
This is a GOOD way!
Hi! My name is Cookie! What's your name?
KER-BONK!
This is NOT a good way!
New friends can be very different from you...
DIRT! WEIRD!
OVEN! SCARY!
...but that's what makes them interesting!

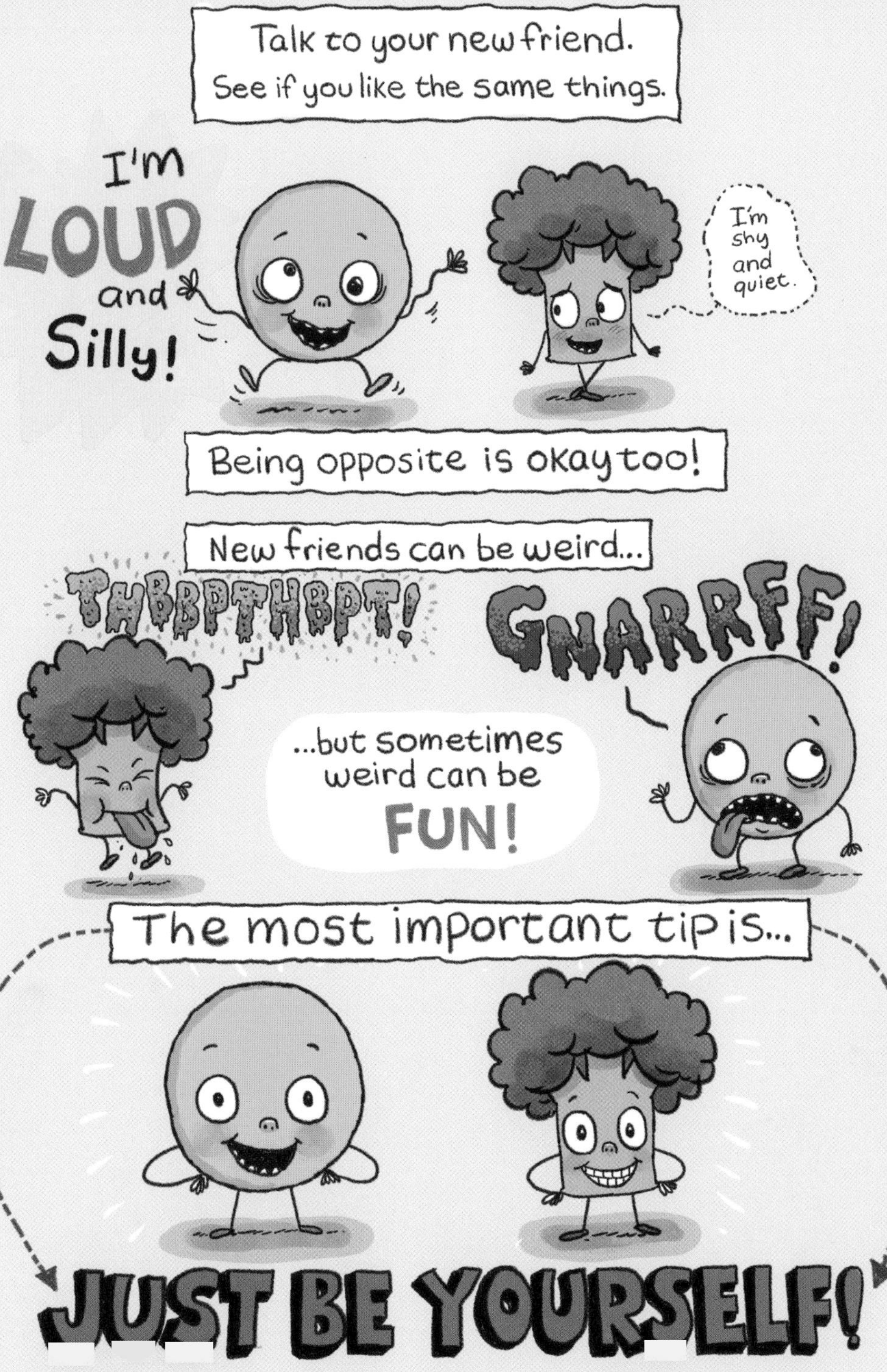

Talk to your new friend.
See if you like the same things.
I'm LOUD and Silly!
I'm shy and quiet.
Being opposite is okay too!
New friends can be weird...
THBBPTHBPT!
GNARRFF!
...but sometimes weird can be FUN!
The most important tip is...
JUST BE YOURSELF!

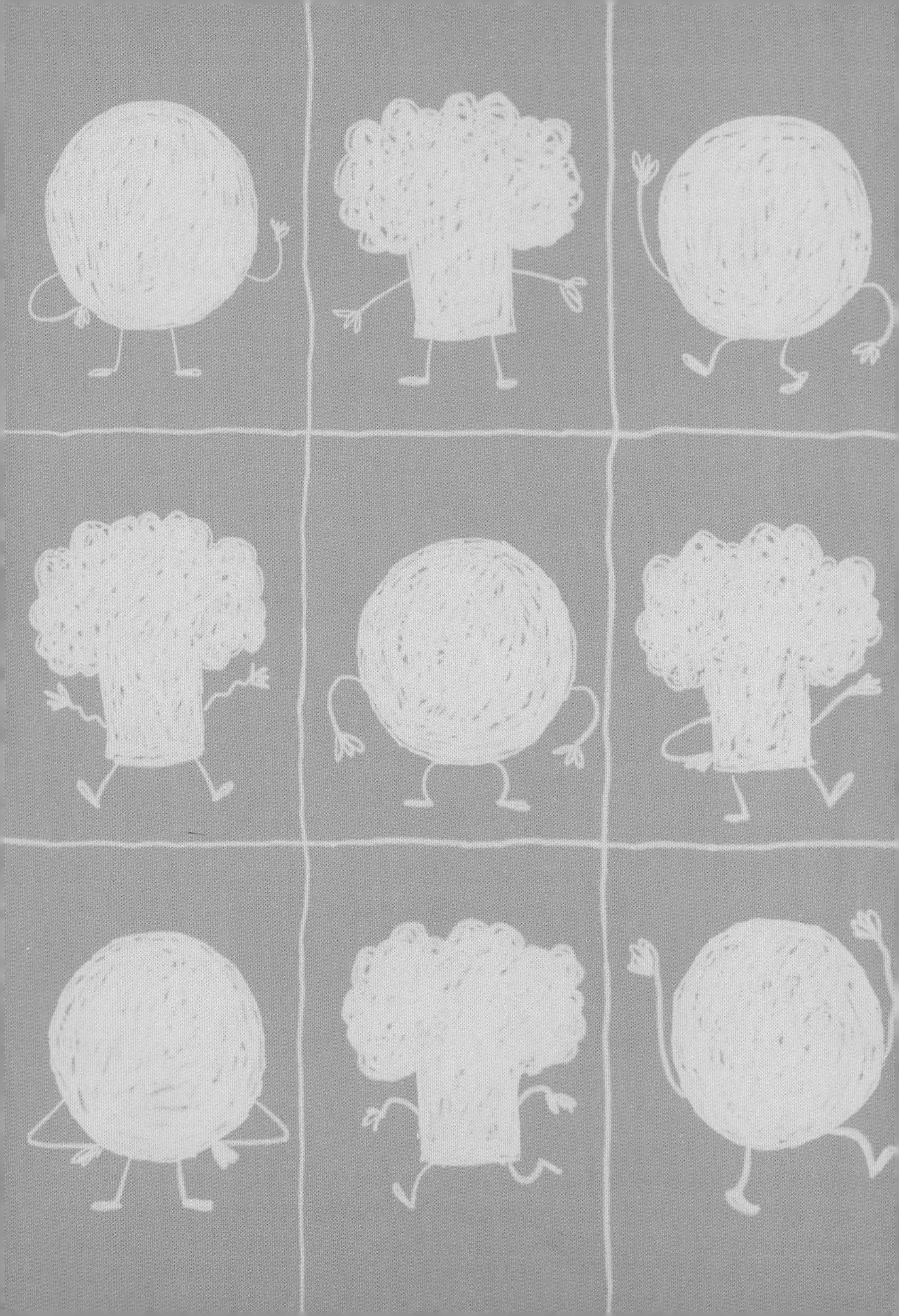

Epilogue

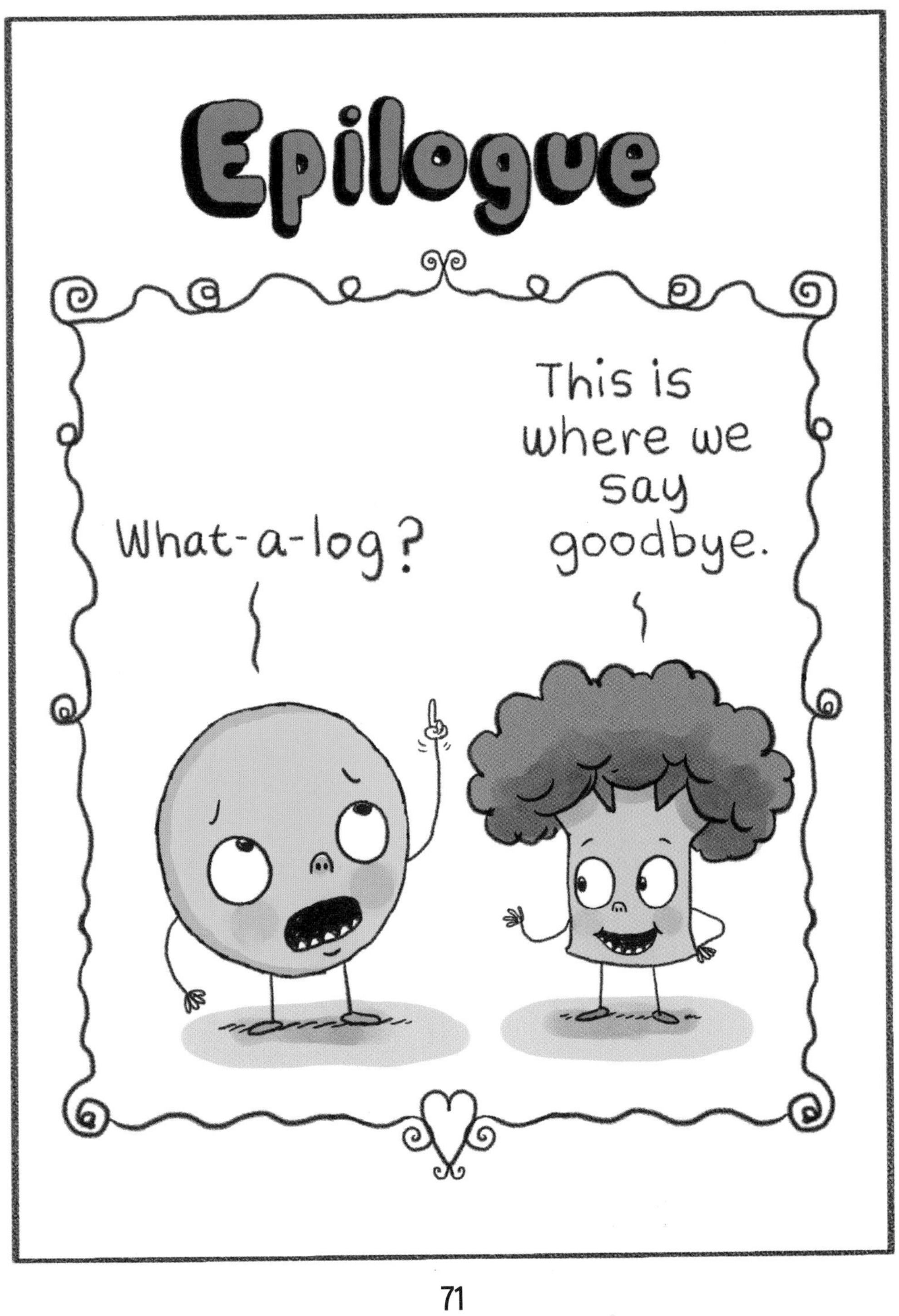

What-a-log?
This is where we say goodbye.

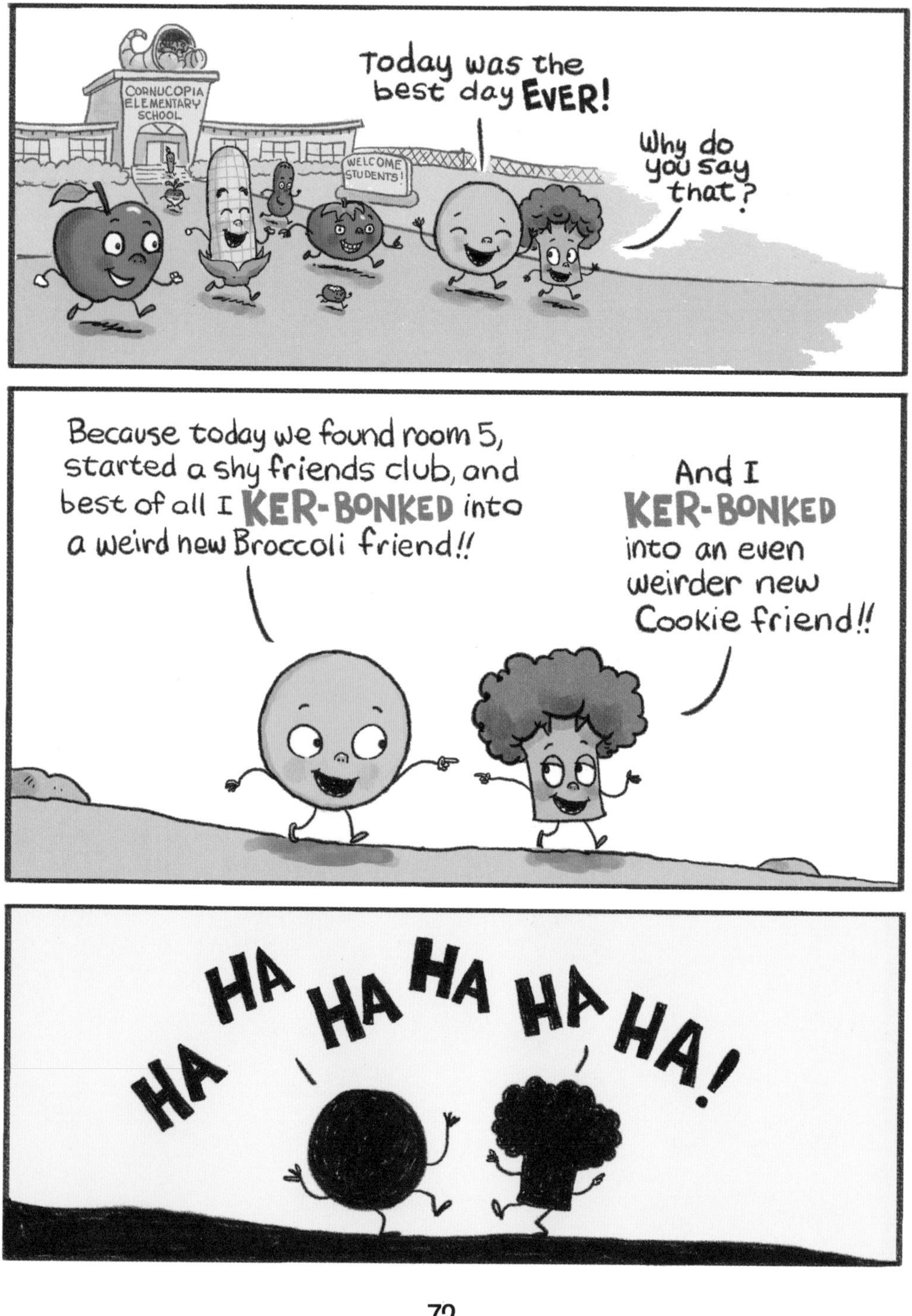
CORNUCOPIA ELEMENTARY SCHOOL
WELCOME STUDENTS!
Today was the best day EVER!
Why do you say that?
Because today we found room 5, started a shy friends club, and best of all I KER-BONKED into a weird new Broccoli friend!!
And I KER-BONKED into an even weirder new Cookie friend!!
HA HA HA HA HA HA HA!

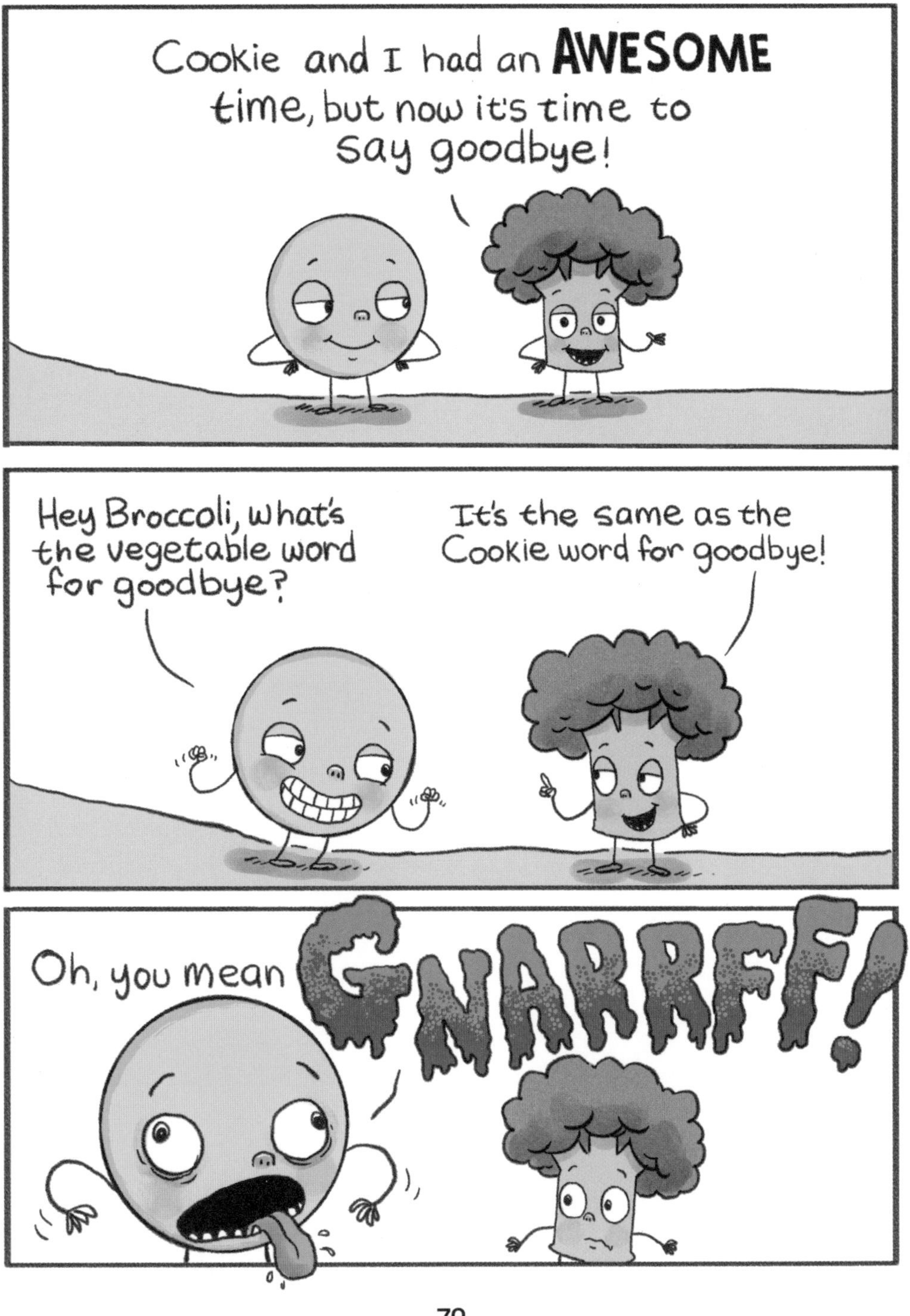
Cookie and I had an AWESOME time, but now it's time to say goodbye!
Hey Broccoli, what's the vegetable word for goodbye?
It's the same as the Cookie word for goodbye!
Oh, you mean
GNARFF!

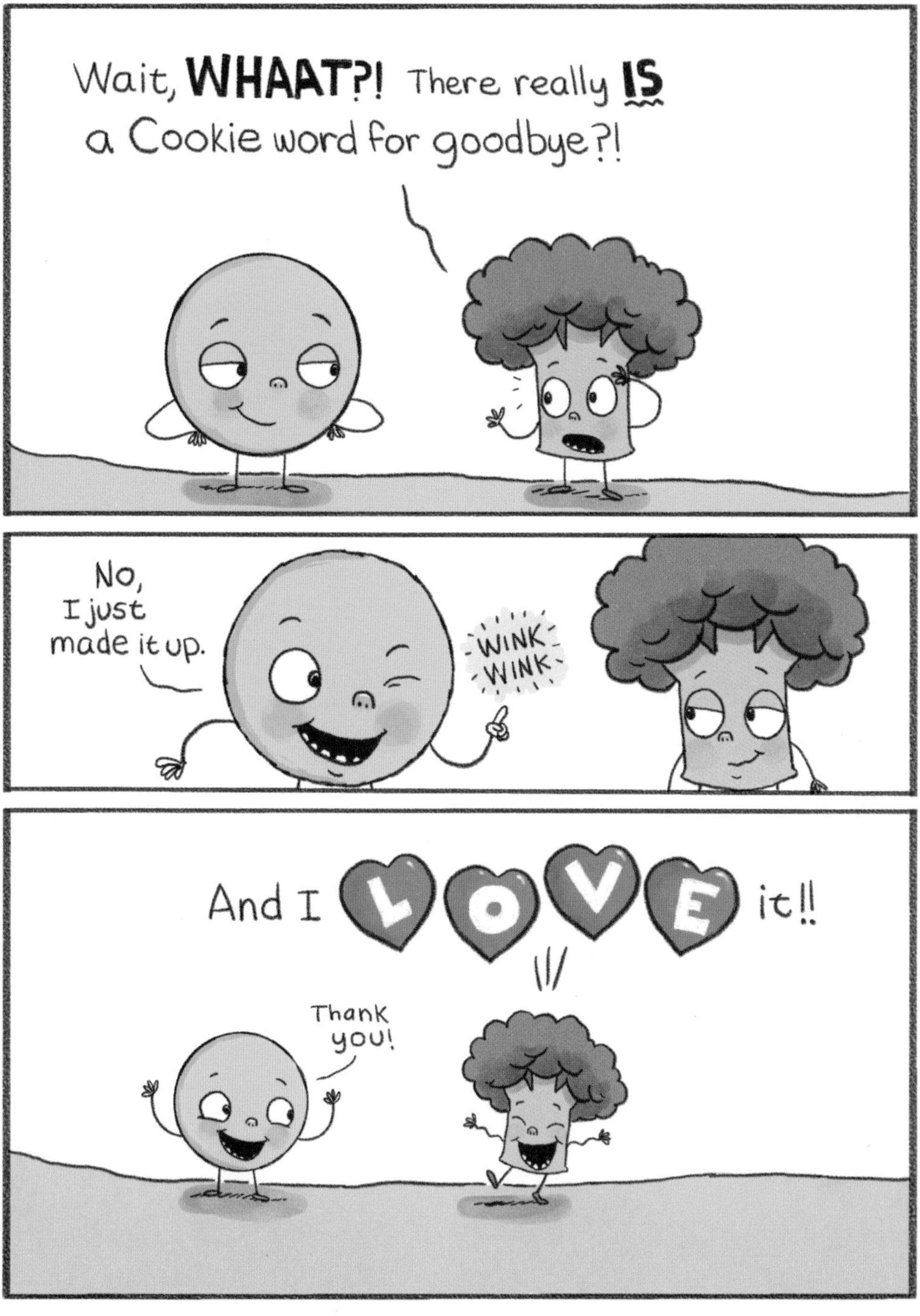
Wait, WHAAT?! There really IS a Cookie word for goodbye?!
No, I just made it up.
WINK WINK
And I LOVE it!!
Thank you!

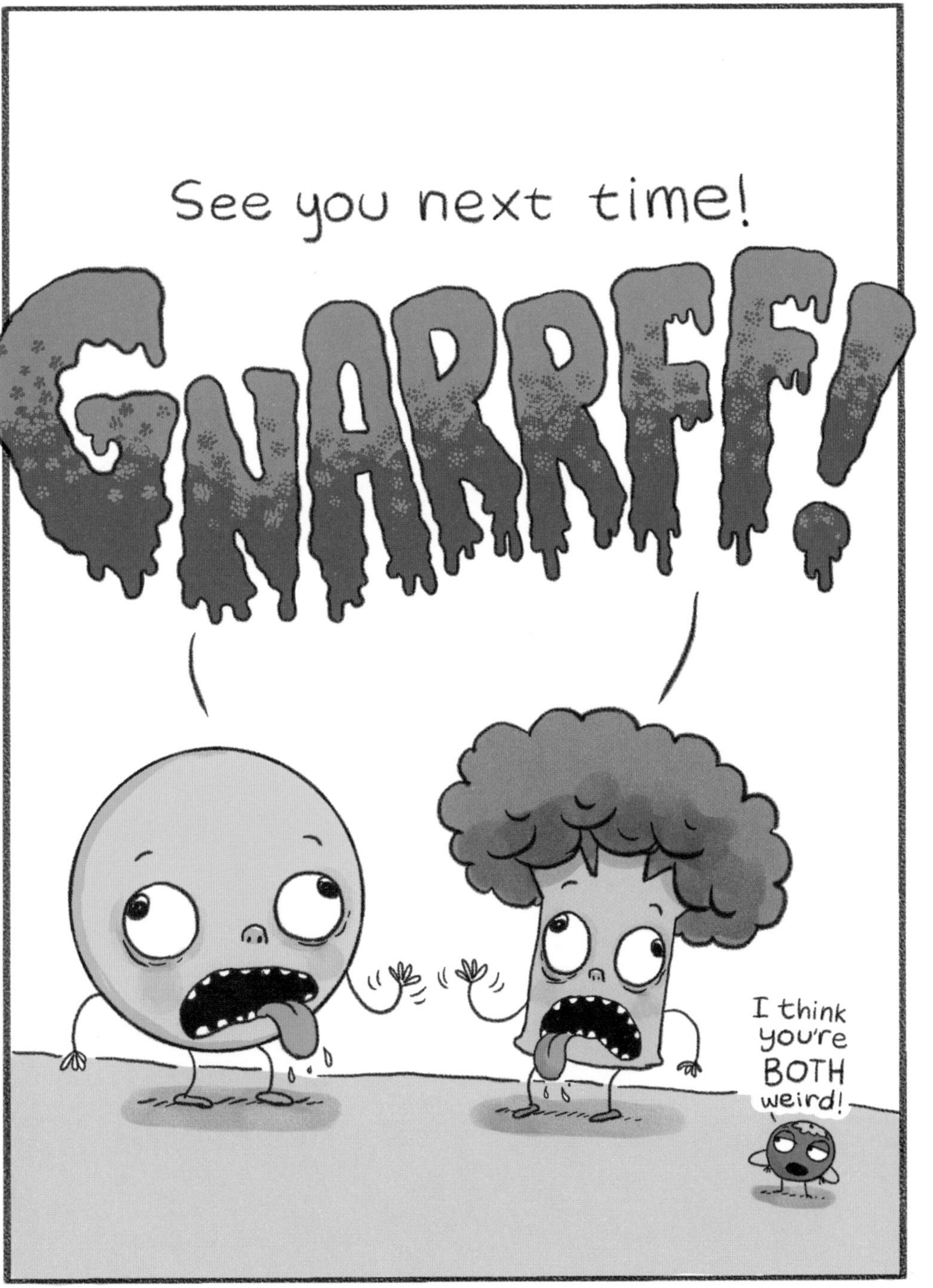
See you next time!
GNARFF!
I think you're BOTH weird!

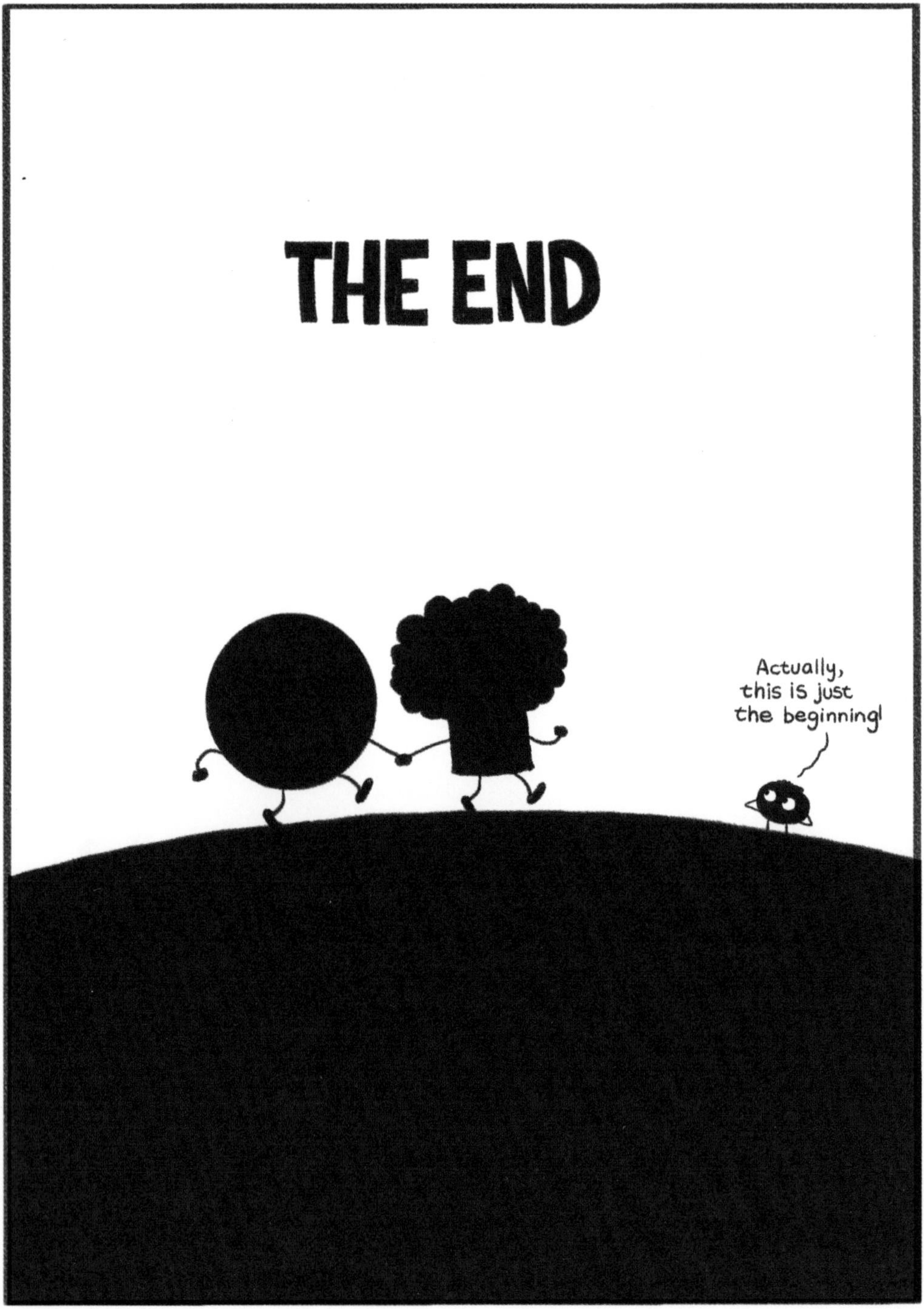
THE END
Actually, this is just the beginning!